Take Me To The Mountain

Modern Mail Order Bride, Mountain Man Romance

Kaci Rose

Five Little Roses Publishing

Copyright

Copyright © 2022, by Kaci Rose, Five Little Roses Publishing. All Rights Reserved.

No part of this publication may be reproduced, distributed,
or transmitted in any form or by any means, including photocopying, recording,
or other electronic or mechanical methods, or by any information storage and
retrieval system without the prior written permission of the publisher, except
in the case of very brief quotations embodied in critical reviews and certain
other noncommercial uses permitted by copyright law.

Publisher's Note: This is a work of fiction. Names,

characters, places, and incidents are a product of the author's imagination.

Locales and public names are sometimes used for atmospheric purposes. Any

resemblance to actual people, living or dead, or to businesses, companies,

events, institutions, or locales is completely coincidental.

Book Cover By: **Wildheart Graphics**

Editing By: Debbe @ **On The Page, Author and PA Services**

Proofread By: Ashley @ **Geeky Girl Author Services**

Contents

Dedication	VII
Blurb	IX
Get Free Books!	XI
1. Chapter 1	1
2. Chapter 2	11
3. Chapter 3	19
4. Chapter 4	32
5. Chapter 5	45
6. Chapter 6	55
7. Chapter 7	61
8. Chapter 8	71
9. Chapter 9	79
10. Chapter 10	88
11. Chapter 11	95
12. Chapter 12	109
13. Chapter 13	121

14.	Chapter 14	127
15.	Chapter 15	137
16.	Chapter 16	146
17.	Chapter 17	159
18.	Chapter 18	170
19.	Chapter 19	179
20.	Chapter 20	187
21.	Chapter 21	194
22.	Chapter 22	204
23.	Chapter 23	211
24.	Epilogue	225
25.	Other Books by Kaci Rose	233
26.	Connect with Kaci Rose	237
	About Kaci Rose	239
	Please Leave a Review!	241

Dedication

To all those who ever think of running off to the mountain and leaving everyday life behind, even just for a weekend.

Blurb

My mountain man just had a delivery mailed to his door. Me.

Willow:

I was out of options when I signed up for the website. Now I'm a modern day mail-order bride and I've been delivered to the doorstep of my mountain man groom.

Bennett is a gentle giant who tells me that he knew I was his from the moment he saw me. I'm on the run from my past, and the mountain man's bed is the best place to stay hidden.

I just need my secrets to stay hidden too.

Bennett:

She's a tiny slip of a thing that I can lift one-handed, but my new bride is a spitfire too. From the moment I saw her, I knew I would do anything to protect her.

And nobody messes with what is mine.

Our marriage has been consummated in body, but I intend to have her heart and soul too. And that means that my sweet bride has to tell me everything. Even her darkest secrets.

Now that I have her, I won't let her go. And anyone who threatens our life together is going to have a giant problem on their hands.

Me.

Get Free Books!

Do you like Military Men? Best friends brothers?
What about sweet, sexy, and addicting books?

If you join Kaci Rose's Newsletter you get these books free!

https://www.kacirose.com/free-books/

Now on to the story!

Chapter 1

Willow

I grew up in a small town just outside of Chicago, and I thought going into the city would be the most adventure I'd have in my life. Boy, was I wrong.

If only my dad could see me now taking a bus across the country to meet a guy I did not know, who I will be marrying in just two weeks or less. That alone would probably kill him if he wasn't already dead.

When my dad lost his battle with cancer, his savings couldn't cover all of his medical bills and funeral costs. With the sale of our house, I was able to pay those expenses. But that left me effectively homeless, and with what happened at the funeral, I needed to get out of town and fast.

After staying in a women's shelter for a week, my friend Aspen allowed me to crash at her place. Like me, her mother had just passed away from cancer and was looking for a way to make some money so she could keep her house.

She ended up at Club Red selling her virginity in an auction. I keep thinking about her and wondering how it's going. But I, on the other hand, decided to look into this mail-order bride website that one of the ladies had talked about at the women's shelter.

So, right now I'm on my way to meet my future husband whose name is Bennett. We've talked through email, and I know that he lives on a mountain in a small town called Whiskey River located in Montana. Apparently, it's not easy to meet girls and with his friends, all married he decided to take an unconventional approach to find his wife.

I figure a tiny town up on a mountain that's really hard to find seems like a perfect place to be safe, and maybe I'll be able to let my guard down again for the first time in months.

After the contracts were signed, Bennett sent me more than enough money to get out to Whiskey River, cover any of my food and costs along the way, and have plenty left over.

I had no idea that mail-order websites still existed outside of the Old West novels that my dad used to read. But now I guess it's just a different type of dating with all those reality shows. You know the ones where they know someone for ninety days or less and get married before they even meet the person.

Once I arrive at the bus stop, the photos I have of Bennett are the only way I'll know how to find him. We agreed to meet a few towns over so that we're not drawing any attention to ourselves in Whiskey River with it being such a small town and all.

When I look into his dark brown eyes in the photos, they appear kind and my dad always said that a person's eyes are a window to their soul. But let's be honest, he's not bad looking either. His hair is a bit long and you can tell that he's used to hard work based on the muscles he has, as I'm sure any mountain man is.

Though I was nervous about the thought of living up on the mountain, he assures me he doesn't need me for the hard work. The house would be my domain. I can take care of the cooking, cleaning, and decorating while he would provide for us and any of our future family.

As the mountains start coming into view, my nerves kick into gear. And not for the first time, the thoughts start racing through my head. Is there any other possible way to do this without marrying a stranger? Yet nothing comes to mind.

Finally, I try to distract myself by reading one of the books that I picked up for a quarter at the local library sale before heading out of town. At last, we reach my bus stop and I sit there and look out the window for a moment trying to spot Bennett.

It's easy to spot him as he's taller than most people and sticks out in the crowd. Though he does look almost exactly like his picture as he stands there with his arms crossed, staring at the bus with a blank expression on his face.

At the last moment, I think that I could stay on the bus and drive to the next town, get a different ticket, and shoot him an email in a few days apologizing. Heck, maybe that's what I should do. But my dad taught me that when you give your word you follow through always. So, I stand up and gather my bag as I make my way to the front of the bus.

Though Bennett can't see into the bus because the windows are tinted, I can still see him and his eyes are glued to the door of the bus. Hesitating for just a moment, I step out to meet him.

The moment our eyes lock, his expression softens and his arms drop. Slowly he makes his way over to me and offers a very forced smile.

"Willow," he says, but it's not a question

I simply nodded my head.

"Bags?" he asks.

Yet again I nod.

We walk over to where they're unloading bags from the extra storage area in the bus. When I see mine, I reach for it, but he places his hand on mine and stops me. Then, picking up my bag as if it weighs nothing, he places his arm around my back, carefully guiding me to the parking lot.

Even though he's slightly awkward, I find it absolutely adorable. Actually, it helps settle my nerves quite a bit. Then he guides me out to a truck that's obviously well-used and covered in dirt. When he opens the door, I find the inside clean, which is the exact opposite of what I was expecting.

He takes my bags and places them in the back and then helps me into my seat. However, he doesn't close the door until I'm buckled in. While he walks to his side, it gives me a minute to take a deep breath, and recenter myself.

"Ready to head home?" he asks once he is in his seat.

It may not feel like home, but I guess it is going to be my home. Isn't it? Though it's hard to think of a place I've never seen before as home.

"Yes, I'll be happy to get there." Then I give him as much of a smile as I can because he's been nothing shy of a perfect gentleman.

He puts the truck in gear and navigates out of town onto a small two-lane highway as we head out of town.

"Will you tell me about Whiskey River?" I ask, wanting to know about where I will be living.

"I think you'll like it here. The people are really friendly. We have a small downtown area where there are some stores, including a bakery and a café. Throughout the year, the town has a few events, which we can go to if you'd like. I know it's not Chicago, but I promise we can find you plenty to do here, too." He says, glancing my way.

So basically, it's the typical small town. It will take some getting used to, but if it means not looking over my shoulder constantly, I say it's a fair tradeoff.

"If I wanted Chicago, I would have stayed there. Small town life seems perfect right now and I can't wait to see Whiskey River." I offer him a smile that seems to relax him.

Once we get close to Whiskey River, he lets me know, and we drive right down Main Street. Right in front of us is a huge mountain that you could see when walking down the street. The whole downtown has a very cute mountain town vibe with rustic wood and stones.

Main Street seems to have everything from a thrift store to a little grocery store, a café, a bakery, an outdoor store, the bank, and more. It doesn't take us long to drive through downtown, and we are heading out of town and up towards the mountain.

"Come winter it'll be harder to get into town. But the upside is we'll be able to do winter sports if that's something you're interested in," he says.

"I've always wanted to go sledding, but I've never been," I tell him.

"Sledding we can do. Not too far from the house, there's a really great hill perfect for sledding."

As we continue on the way up to his place, there are some amazing views of the mountain and the scenery below. When we turn into his driveway, it's still a long way up to the actual cabin, but when we break through the trees, I couldn't stop the gasp if I wanted to.

His house looks more like a resort with a breathtaking vista of the mountains in the background. It looks like an upscale rustic ski lodge that you would see in a magazine. There are large windows all over the house, taking full advantage of the view. To the side of the house is a garden and then on the other side of the cleared area are some outbuildings and what looks like a large barn.

"This is your house?" I ask completely shocked.

"Yes, I wanted to take advantage of the view." He seems a little nervous again.

"It's absolutely stunning. I was seriously picturing a little cabin in the woods."

When he smiles this time, I can tell it's a fully genuine smile. My heart skips a beat at how truly beautiful this man is when he smiles.

He gets out of the truck and grabs my bags, and opens the door for me. I take a deep breath and step foot on the mountain that I will be calling home.

Chapter 2

Bennett

Entering the cabin, I take a deep breath, watching her for any sign of how she feels about it. I know she liked the outside, but it is still a man's cabin. I never thought when I built and decorated it, I'd be bringing my wife here. Getting married was something I didn't think was in the cards for me up here and I was okay with that.

I stand behind her as she steps into the living room with its tall stone fireplace and large windows that look out over the front of the house. Behind the living room is a dining room and also a decent-sized kitchen. All the windows are equally large and full of natural light.

When she finally turns to look back at me, she has a huge smile on her face.

"This is absolutely gorgeous, Bennett," she says, and I let out a breath I didn't even realize I was holding.

On the mail-order bride website, when I saw her photo, I knew that this girl was mine. The feeling is ten times stronger in person. I need to remember to thank my friend Axel's wife, Emelie, the next time I see them. If she hadn't suggested an online dating website, I wouldn't have even been on the computer browsing when I came across the website that held Willow's profile.

It seems like it took forever for her to get here, and I didn't know if she was safe or if she was going to just back out altogether. Even though I like my solitude here on the mountain, if she had tried to back out, I would have had to go after her.

Now, after seeing her in person, hearing her voice, and having her smell fill my truck, those feelings are so much more intense.

According to our contract, we have two weeks to get to know each other before we make the decision to get married or go our separate ways. So, she still has the chance to back out, and I sure as hell don't want that. Instead, I want to show her all the reasons that she should stay and choose to be with me. Starting with the fact that there's plenty to do here, even though we seem to be a small town.

"There's a rodeo in town. Would you like to go with me tomorrow night?" I ask, even though tomorrow night is Friday night and probably going to be the busiest day of the rodeo.

"I've never been to a rodeo. So yes, I'd like that very much."

"Then, on Saturday, my friend Axel and his wife Emelie would like to have us over for dinner along with three other couples. They all want to meet you. The guys are good friends of mine, and they all live up here on the mountain. They are our support group." While I don't want to overwhelm her, I do want her to meet people too. The last thing I want is for her to ever feel like she's isolated.

"I'd really like to meet your friends," she says as she sets her bag down on the bed and takes a look around the room.

The walls are the raw logs that you see on the outside of the house. There are wood floors with some animal skin rugs, a large handmade bed with animal skin blankets on it, and an attached closet in the bathroom.

"Sunday, I'll show you around the land, and then come Monday, we could go into town, maybe have lunch and get you a dress for Cash and Hope's wedding next week." I know I'm rambling, but I figure if I give her enough to do, maybe she'll feel like this is her home and someplace she wants to stay.

"That sounds like fun." She smiles again, and I know we're both nervous. This is completely out of my wheelhouse, and I'm sure she feels the same as well.

"This dresser over here is yours, and half the closet is cleaned out and ready for you. Also, there are hangers in there for you to use. You have your own sink in the bathroom and a set of drawers next to the sink where you can store anything you need. There's a closet in the bathroom with towels and things, and there's a spot in the shower for you to place your stuff. Anything that you brought is free to be anywhere in the house. This is your home now, so put your stamp on it."

After giving her a short tour of the room, I leave to make dinner and give her a little bit of space to unpack and settle in.

Though I want nothing more than to be at her side, I know it's the right thing to do to give her some time alone. And as much as I hate the idea, I will sleep on the couch for a few days.

As I go over all the different places in my head that I want to show her on Sunday, she steps into the kitchen and sits down on one of the bar stools.

"What do you expect of me now that I'm here?" she asks.

It's a fair question. When I was talking with the woman in charge of the website, she said many men order a mail-order bride to run their household, cook dinner, help clean the house, and be at their side for different events.

So, I'm sure this is what she was expecting. "The house is yours to do with as you wish. If you would like to redecorate, that is all up to you. I want it to feel like your home. But I will help cook and clean as I don't expect you to do all of it. What I do expect is for you to learn how to stay safe out here and how to help with winter prep so that you are able to fend for yourself if needed. In the winter, it can be dangerous out here, and the more you know, the safer you will be." I tell her honestly.

"I can do that. How long have you been living up here on the mountain?"

"Just over eight years now. The first few were spent building the house and learning how to survive up here. Now, it's more about learning how to keep busy."

As we eat dinner, knowing that I cooked the food that she was eating gives me a sense of pride that I can take care of her. It's an odd feeling and something I've never really felt before.

After dinner, she helps with the dishes before a huge yawn takes over.

"You've had a long day. Why don't you head to the bedroom and try to get some sleep? Daylight comes early around here. I'll sleep on the couch and give you a little space." I tell her.

"It's your bedroom. I should be the one on the couch," she says with a shocked look on her face.

"Not negotiable. I'm hoping you will agree to be my wife at the end of these few weeks and know I will always take care of you. That means I will take the couch. I'll be on the couch until you are comfortable enough to have me in bed with you, I'll be on the couch."

She hesitates, and I get the feeling that she wants to argue. Finally, her eyes flit over my face before she agrees.

"Okay. Thank you. I'll see you in the morning."

I watch her go to bed before checking every door and window in the house to make sure it's all sealed up. This is not a routine I normally have when it's just me.

But tonight feels different.

Chapter 3

Willow

Even though I didn't sleep very well last night, I still slept much better than I have in weeks. At least for now, I feel a lot safer out here. I know he slept on the couch because he wanted to be a gentleman, but I couldn't tell him without raising suspicions that I'd feel much safer with him in bed with me. The last thing I need is for him to find out what I'm running from and tell me to hit the road.

He'd be completely justified in doing so.

Hearing him outside chopping wood, I take the time to really look around the house and get a feel for my surroundings. For being secluded up on the mountain and self-sufficient, it's a lot more modern than I expected.

The kitchen looks like it could be set in any home. The countertops are granite with a modern feel. He has a refrigerator, a microwave, and even a dishwasher. But then there's a classic wood-burning stove.

Next to the kitchen is a decent-sized laundry room with a sink, counters, and a washer and dryer. I guess I thought he would have been hand-washing his clothes. But the most surprising find of all is that he has a telephone in the living room. It looks like an old dial-up telephone that I had in my house growing up before cell phones were as big as they are. When I pick up the handset, there's a dial tone. I'll have to see if he's willing to give me the number so Aspen can call and check in when she's safe.

The cabin has four bedrooms, but he uses one of the bedrooms as an office. Another one is set up like a library, and then there's a second almost guest bedroom, but it doesn't have a bed, just some dressers and storage cabinets. Then there's the primary bedroom I slept in last night.

In the spare bedroom, I find a box of old, worn-out t-shirts. Most of them have holes in them, but they're in decent enough shape that they would make a great t-shirt quilt. Also, there's a sewing machine in the living room, so I can use it to show him I can be useful around the house. One of my winter projects could be to make a quilt out of these t-shirts.

It's a win-win because I love to quilt. I haven't had the opportunity to do so since my dad died and even before then because I was just too busy taking care of him. So, I pick up the box, take it into the living room, and set it next to the sewing machine. I check the drawers in the machine and find all the thread that I need.

While he's outside doing his chores, this can be one of the things I'm doing in the house.

By the time he comes inside to get ready for the rodeo, I have a smile on my face. That I'll be helping to contribute to the house, even in a small way, makes me feel a lot better about being here.

"Let me know when you're ready, and we can get going," he says as he comes out of the bathroom in a nice pair of jeans and a button-down shirt.

He looks downright mouthwatering with his muscular body on display. I'm sure he'd have no problem getting girls at an event like a rodeo, which makes me wonder why a hot guy like him did the mail-order bride thing.

I head into the bathroom and put on a pair of jeans, a comfortable but dressier t-shirt, and a pair of sneakers that I wouldn't mind getting dirty. After putting a few curls into my hair, I swipe on a little mascara and lip gloss before leaving the room.

When I step out, his eyes find me immediately. His eyes dance over my face before taking in the entire length of my body and then slowly travel back up and locking with my eyes.

"You look beautiful," he says as he clears his throat.

Then he opens the front door for me, and he's the perfect gentleman. Just like yesterday, he opens my car door and makes sure I'm settled in the truck before going around to his side.

When we're in the truck, he turns the radio on low for some background noise before smiling back at me.

"My friends and their wives are going to be there. They'll come over and say hi, but they'll let us be today, but tomorrow they will want to talk to both of us," he says as I look out the window.

"Will you tell me about them so at least I can say that I've heard about them?" I ask.

This earns me a huge smile. I guess he likes that I'm actually taking an interest in his friends and his life.

"There's Axel and his wife, Emelie. They were the first to get married, and I'll let you hear their story from them. But he's a pretty big guy, so don't be alarmed when you see him. She's the sweetest person you will ever meet. She makes sure to take care of me and always sends me home with food when she sees me. Then there's Jenna and Phoenix. They were the next to get married. He's a talented woodworker and makes a lot of the wood furniture you'll see in town and some of the furniture in my place. She's a photographer specializing in national parks and sells her photos in town and online.

Then there is Hope and Cash, whose wedding we're going to. And finally, there is Jana and Cole, who live on the land bordering Cash and Hope. Cole has been somewhat of a recluse. He's a great guy, and only just joined our group. He's got a scar on the side of his face, but don't let it startle you. This will be his first big event with crowds, so give him a little leeway."

I appreciate that he gave me a heads up on Cole and that he's protective of the rest of them as well. It says a lot about who he is and how loyal he is to his friends. Hopefully, maybe one day, I'll fall into the category of deserving that kind of loyalty from him, too.

The rest of the car ride, he talks about some of the rodeos he's gone to in the past and what I can expect since it's my first time.

No sooner are we inside the gates of the rodeo than a group of people head right for us.

"You must be Willow! We're so excited to meet you. I'm Emelie, and this is my husband, Axel," the little blonde one says.

They take turns introducing themselves, and it's overwhelming trying to remember everyone's names. But like Bennett promised, they don't crowd us.

"Tomorrow, we will see you both for lunch." The blonde one says again, and then they go grab their seats.

"Let's get some seats over there," Bennett says as we walk in the opposite direction of his friends.

Even though his friends seemed really nice, I find meeting new people can be quite intense. Thankfully, he seems to understand, as do his friends, by giving us our space.

I didn't quite know what to expect with the rodeo, but there are people everywhere, and I can easily tell that he is uncomfortable. Bennett's trying to hide it, but I don't blame him because this whole place makes me feel uneasy, too.

Grabbing seats in the metal bleachers a few rows up from the front, we're so close we can smell the dirt ring below us and the food that's in the air.

I'm enjoying watching the barrel racers, and the girls on the horses are just amazing.

Leaning over, nodding towards the horses in the ring in front of us, he asks, "Do you know how to ride?"

"Not very well. I've gone a few times with some friends, but that's about it."

"I'll teach you. It will come in handy out here."

Then we go back to watching the show before he turns back to me again.

"Are you hungry? I can go grab some food," he says.

I panic just a little as I don't want to be left alone, and he seems to sense it.

"You can come with me and see what they have," he suggests, and I nod.

As we're looking at the food options, it's very hard not to notice all the girls that stare at him. Some of them walk by and giggle, but when I look at him, it's like he doesn't even realize they're paying him so much attention.

Maybe he's just being polite with me here and all. I shake my head and try to focus on the food choices in front of me.

"Don't pay them any attention." He leans down and whispers into my ear.

"So, you did notice them." I try to say in a flirty tone with just a hint of a smile.

"No, I noticed how uncomfortable you were and then put two and two together. Most of us moved out here to the mountain for one reason or the other, so we're used to being stared at in crowds for our size or our scars."

"Trust me, that's not why they're staring." I shake my head but get in line to grab a hot dog.

"Their opinion doesn't matter. What matters is if you like what you see," he says, completely shocking me.

Taking the opportunity, I run my eyes over him as slowly as he did me when I stepped out of the bedroom earlier.

"Yeah, I like what I see," I tell him honestly.

That seems to be all he needs because he relaxes and wraps an arm around my waist as we wait in line together. Though it's a small gesture, it signals that I'm his now, and he's mine. Even if it's only by a contract.

We get our food and go back to our seats just as the bull riding gets ready to start. Watching these men try to go for eight seconds on a prancing bull is pure madness.

These animals weigh so much that when their feet hit the ground I can feel the vibration in my seat. Every time one of the men gets thrown to the ground, my heart stops until I know they're okay.

Finally, I begin to relax and enjoy myself until I see a photographer walking closer to us, taking photos of the crowd. Inching closer to Bennett, I bury my face in his arm when she aims her camera our way. He shifts, wraps his arm around me, and pulls me into his side, allowing me to hide.

The last thing I need is for a picture of me to go public and show exactly where I am. My uncle will be looking for things like that, so I have to be careful. If Bennett picks up on it, I'm hoping he thinks I simply don't enjoy having my picture taken.

"She's gone. You okay?" he says after a few minutes.

I'm not, and thankfully he doesn't push the subject any further, at least not right now. Though I'm sure I'll hear about it once we get home.

The rest of the night goes smoothly. We leave before the rodeo is over to avoid most of the traffic in the parking lot. On the way home, he keeps the topics light but looks over at me like he's expecting me not to be okay or for something else to come up. I am unsure what to say or do, so I keep trying to offer a reassuring smile.

"I had a really good time tonight," he says when we get to the front door.

"So did I," I tell him. Because despite being uncomfortable and for that roaming photographer trying to take a picture, I really did have a good time.

He smiles and places a hand on my hip as he gently drops a soft kiss on my lips. I've dated before, and I've been kissed before, but holy hell, nothing has felt quite like Bennett's lips on mine.

The kiss is soft and a bit unsure, like he's expecting me to pull away. One thing I do know, it's way too short. Does it mean anything that he's the one that pulls away first?

My heart's racing like I just ran a marathon, and my lips tingle where his were touching mine. Even though his eyes are heated and he's acting like he wants more, he takes a step back. Then, like nothing happened, he opens the door and we go inside.

"Goodnight, Willow. If you need me, I'll be here on the couch."

I want to ask him to come to bed or even just stay here until I fall asleep, but the thought of having to tell him why terrifies me. So once again, I head to bed alone.

Chapter 4

Bennett

It's the morning after the rodeo, and we're just sitting down to have breakfast together. Though I could tell something was up last night, I didn't feel like it was the right time to bring it up. I want her to trust me and feel like she can open up to me, and I know that will come in time. Even still, I have this feeling I can't shake that something's wrong.

"I was wondering, and don't feel like you have to answer if you don't want to," I say. "But I was curious why you did this mail-order bride thing," I ask, hoping to get some insight.

"I was raised by my father. When I was really young, my mom took off, though she was never really in the picture. During my senior year in high school, my dad got cancer and fought hard. It went into remission, but we were left with a stack of bills. Both of us worked hard to pay them off, but then the cancer came back and this time, he lost his battle. With the sale of the house, I was left with just enough money to cover his debt, but I had nothing. After the..."

She stops and clears her throat. "After the funeral, I moved in to a women's shelter for a while, and one of the women there told me about the website. I figured with everything going on; it was best to get out of town."

Listening to her, it's very clear she's hiding something, but she's not comfortable telling me whatever it is. The last thing I want to do is pressure her and push her further away. Whatever she's hiding, it doesn't matter because she's here with me. And what matters the most is she's safe with me.

I'll do everything in my power to keep her safe. Though it would be much easier if I knew what I was up against. No matter what it is, she doesn't want to be found. Yesterday, it was obvious by the way she acted toward the photographer taking pictures in our direction. I make a mental note to avoid large crowds like that for the time being.

"What about you? Why did you do it?" she asks.

I was expecting her question, as I can't ask something of her I am not willing to share myself.

"Emelie, who you met last night, tried to get me on a few online dating websites. Since I'm the last one of us not married, I think she saw something in my eyes when I watched them. I have to admit that I want what they have badly.

But I didn't like the website that she shared. Then I went down a black hole of different websites and somehow ended up on the mail-order bride one. I thought it was interesting because I didn't realize they still did the mail-order bride thing anymore. So, I decided to take a look, and your picture caught my eye, and it was just something about you."

"Me?" she asks, a little shocked.

"Yes, you. Even from your picture, I felt this connection that I couldn't explain. The feeling was even stronger when I saw you get off the bus."

Hopefully, I'm not scaring her off, but I want her to know I'm telling the truth. She studies me for a bit, like she wants to say something, but she's not sure she should. Then, not quite meeting my eyes, she offers me a smile.

"I feel safe around you, and that's saying a lot because I haven't felt safe since my dad passed."

I tuck that little bit of information away because I feel like it's going to be useful in trying to figure her out.

But I'm glad she feels safe, and I'll make sure that when I'm around she continues to feel protected at all costs.

Even though the rest of breakfast is comfortable and the conversation is all about getting to know each other, something in the back of my head is uneasy. I can't help wondering what she needs to feel safe from and how I can make her feel completely protected and secure again.

After breakfast, I head out to do some chores with the animals, and she stays inside to clean up and do whatever else she has decided to do to keep her busy.

Though I hated being at the rodeo with all those people, she seemed to have a good time. Well, except for the photographer. But until I know what she's running from and how to protect her, I think it's best to keep her away from crowds. I can talk to the guys tonight and get their opinion.

And then tomorrow we can have a nice relaxing day, and I can show her the property. The top of my list is to ensure she knows at least the basics of getting around and where she can normally find me.

Once I'm done, I go inside to take a shower and get ready.

When she steps out in jeans and a t-shirt that's nice and simple and makes her curves pop and her long legs stand out, she looks absolutely stunning. Her light brown hair frames her face perfectly.

While she seems slightly nervous on the way to Emelie's house, I assume it's because she's meeting new people. But we both know they're going to be asking a ton of questions.

"I was thinking maybe we just tell people that we met on an online dating website and leave the mail-order bride part out of it," I tell her as we're driving.

At first, she doesn't say anything. But then she looks over at me. "I think that's for the best. It means fewer questions, and we can always tell them later if we want to. They're your friends, so I'll let you make that decision."

"Well, I'm hoping over time they'll become your friends too," I tell her honestly. Then hesitantly, I reach for her hand, trying to offer some encouragement.

"I hope so, too. Making friends was never easy for me."

We are the last ones to get to Axel and Emelie's. Even though this is where everyone tends to meet, their place is harder to get to since you have to park and then walk up their driveway instead of being able to park the car right by the house.

As we reach the door, I pick up on her nerves, so I wrap my arm around her waist to give her some comfort and strength.

"The guests of honor have arrived! Come in, come in." Emelie greets us at the door with a warm smile and a hug for both of us.

There's another quick round of introductions so Willow can put a name to everyone's face again. The girls head off to the kitchen area to do their thing, and the guys gather in the living room where we can still watch our girls but have a separate conversation.

We begin by planning a group hunting trip. It'll be the first time we do something like this. Normally, each of us hunts for ourselves and at our own speed. But I do like the idea of going out in a group and having a little interaction with each other. It also appeals to me because we can get to know each other better and possibly learn something from each of the other men. Everybody hunts differently, and up here it's never a bad thing to have too many skills or too many ways to do something.

As they talk, I watch Willow interact with the other girls. Though I can tell she's a little shy, she's smiling and talking, which is a good thing. I can't always pick up on what she's saying, but she does appear hesitant, like she's holding back. Which makes me wonder if it's just because of the way we met or if she's trying to make sure that she doesn't say too much. Or, for all I know, it could be something else.

"You're watching her, trying to figure something out," Cash says, which turns the other guys' attention to me as well.

"Even though I know moving here is a huge change for her, I just can't shake this feeling like she's holding something back," I tell them as honestly as I can.

"How did you two meet?" Phoenix asks.

"Online. Emelie actually recommended a few online dating places that I checked out. I found her on one of them and we kind of clicked. Almost instantly from seeing her, I knew that she was the one. For me, it was something I felt in my gut."

"And you said she's your wife at the store a couple of weeks ago?" Axel asks because I did say that.

"She's going to be. We're not married yet. I wanted her to come to the mountain to make sure this is what she truly wants. If it is, we will be married soon. Cole, we might even beat you to the altar." I joke with him, but he just grins and shakes his head, looking over at his bride-to-be, Jana. Though he doesn't even try to hide the smile that covers his face. Those two are as good as married in everyone's eyes here on the mountain.

When Cash's fiancé, Hope, was kidnapped by her mother, he got Cole, his neighbor, to help get her back. But Hope's mother had also kidnapped her best friend, Jana.

Cole had the same reaction to Jana as I did when I saw Willow the first time. We both had undeniable feelings that these women were ours. Jana had been hurt, so Cole took her back to his place to take care of her, and the two have been inseparable ever since.

"What do you think she is holding back?" Axel asks.

"I honestly have no idea. Really, there wasn't anyone to leave behind in Chicago as her father had died. Even though she had no desire to stay there, I get this feeling that she's running from something. I need her to trust me enough to open up about it."

"Well, if you need us, let us know," Cole says.

I know he means more than just in a friendly way, as he's one of the best trackers I've ever seen. Also, there's Cash, who knows a lot to do with security. Plus, the rest of the guys will help protect my cabin if need be.

Watching Willow interact as the night goes on, she slowly relaxes and begins to enjoy herself.

After we eat, the girls separate to play some card games while us men take over doing the dishes since the ladies cooked.

By the time we get ready to head home, Willow is all smiles.

"Your friends are really great. It makes me miss my friend, Aspen, who is back home," she says, her smile faltering.

"You know you can call her and talk anytime you want, right?" I tell her because this is her home now, and I want her to feel comfortable.

"She was in the middle of... a few things. Maybe I can shoot her an email with the phone number, and she can call when she gets the chance?"

"Of course, next time we're in town, we will stop by Jack's shop. There's a computer that he lets me use, and you can send her an email."

Once we're back inside, she's all smiles again.

"I had a really good time tonight," I tell her as I reach for her. Does she realize that she's leaning into me? I wonder.

"I did too. After a few questions, the girls pretty much accepted me as one of their own. It was really nice."

When I take another step towards her, she wraps her arms around my waist. Standing there, looking at each other for a moment, we're waiting to see what the other is going to do.

When I lean in and kiss her this time it's not hesitant or soft. I have been dying all day to taste her lips again, and I don't want to deny myself anymore.

She is addicting, and she alone could pull me to heaven or hell with just a promise of a taste of her lips.

Wrapping my arms around her, I pull her into me. I'm hard as nails, and I want her to feel me, to know what she does to me. She stands on her tiptoes as if trying to get closer even though there is no space between us.

Needing more and wanting all of her, I back her up and press her against the door before gripping her ass and hoisting her up. She wraps her legs around my waist and holds on without breaking our kiss.

When my tongue brushes hers for the first time, tingles race over my body. I want her more than my next breath, but I want her to know I will always do right by her too. I need her to trust me.

So reluctantly, I pull back, set her down on her feet, and kiss her forehead.

"Get some sleep. Tomorrow we'll go check out some of the mountains," I tell her, and she nods, a bit dazed.

Knowing I put that dazed look on her face is sexy as hell. After she goes to the bedroom and closes the door, I get ready for bed and lie on the couch.

There's one way that I can make her feel safe; hopefully, it will be enough.

Chapter 5

Willow

I'm actually pretty excited to see more of the land around Bennett's cabin. If the view just from his house is any indication, it's got to be absolutely gorgeous. We pack a lunch because he says we will be gone most of the day.

"How do you feel about taking the horses instead of the four wheelers?" Bennett asks. "Even though we could take them, I'd like you to be comfortable on the horses as well."

I am a little nervous about horseback riding, as I've only been a handful of times. Those were the just for fun ones. The kind where you ride for hours and are beyond sore the next day. If he thinks this is something I need to learn, then I will do it.

"That's fine. Just bear with me because I know almost nothing when it comes to horses," I tell him honestly.

A brilliant smile crosses his face. Then we head to the barn that I've yet to see and explore, where he picks out a horse that he assures me should be nice and mellow.

"If you two get along, then this will be your horse. If not, we can try to match you with a different one and if none of them work then we will get you your own horse. We have room for plenty more," he says, as if it's nothing to tell someone that they'll make sure to get you a horse if you don't like any of the ones they already have.

Part of me wonders if this is just how Bennett really is or if he's trying a little too hard. Either way, it's nice to have the attention from him. It seems like he actually cares, but only time will tell.

We load up the horses and head out onto a trail beside the barn.

"A little farther down this trail is a bunch of berry bushes. Even though they're wild berries, they are great to eat. Every year I use them to make jams, jellies, and even food for the animals. By harvesting them, it keeps other animals like bears away. The further we can keep them from the house, the better," he tells me.

I have to agree with him there. I don't like bears much myself.

"Have you ever had one get too close to the cabin?"

"When I was building my cabin, I had a lot of animals that came up. But the noise pretty much scared them off. Now I try to keep it as clear as I can, so that it's not an easy food source. That seems to keep them away."

He points out a perfect field for a picnic spot in the spring when the flowers are all in bloom and a trail that leads to one of his favorite hunting spots.

We walk along a river and talk about how he'll set up some fishing here in a few weeks, how the process works, and the various uses of the fish. At this point, we've been on the horses for a couple of hours, stopping only to let them have some water from the river. I'm getting a little sore and shift in my seat, but of course, it doesn't go unnoticed by Bennett.

"Just a few more minutes. Once we break this tree line, we will be at the lake, and I figure that's where we can have lunch."

I nod because I can definitely use some time off of the saddle. Hopefully, this is something that I'll get used to, especially if we're going to be riding more.

I'm thinking about how sorry I'm going to be tomorrow when we break through the tree line. The stunning view takes my breath away. There's a lake surrounded by mountains that still have snow on the top.

When we come to a stop, he dismounts before walking over to me, taking the reins of my horse and helping me off. It feels good to stretch my legs. While he gets the horses some water and secured, he lets me explore. Then Bennett sets up a picnic for us.

I've never been on a picnic before. But it's everything I would picture from the movies with a blanket on the ground and a basket of food.

As we eat, I take in the view, which is something that you would only see on a postcard or in a book, while wondering where you could actually see it in real life.

"This would be the perfect spot for camping," I say, thinking out loud.

"Do you like to camp?" he asks.

"Oh yeah. My father and I used to go all the time before he got sick. It was our way of getting out of the city. We'd turn off our phones and take time to reconnect with each other."

"Well, we've got some time midweek where we could come out for a night or two and camp. The lake makes for some good swimming. I think it would be a great way for us to talk and get to know each other a little better."

"I'd like that." I smile back at him. I think it'd be the perfect way for us to open up and find out about each other.

Plus, I really do enjoy camping, and it's been a long time since I've gone.

"Do you see that spot on the other side of the lake where the big boulders are stacked in almost a hump shape?" he asks, pointing across the lake.

I nod because it's pretty hard to miss the boulders, as they are pretty freaking huge.

"Directly behind there is a cave. I've had to use it a few times when I've been out hunting and got caught in really bad weather. I make it a point to keep it free of animals and stocked with blankets and some dry wood for a fire. There's also a bear-proof crate in there with some canned foods. When we come camping, I'll take you over there and show it to you. It'll make a nice hike around the lake."

Instant dread settles in the pit of my stomach. Why is he telling me this? He has to know I'm hiding something and that I'm running from something. If he knows that, it means he's going to ask.

I wait for the question I don't want to answer, the one that will send him running and maybe ask me to leave. I don't know if I can trust this man. After all, he moved here for a much more peaceful and simple life.

If he knew my situation, he wouldn't want me here because there's a very good chance I could be the disruption to his peace. Yesterday, his friends were so nice to me. Would they still be if they knew the truth?

What if he asks me to leave? Where the hell would I go? I have absolutely nothing except the two suitcases I came here with and a box of photos that Aspen is storing at her house for me.

I wonder if hitchhiking is still a thing and how far I'd be able to get.

"You okay?" Bennett pulls me from my thoughts with concern written all over his face.

It's then I realize it's been quite a while, and he hasn't asked me the dreaded question.

"Yes, just got lost in my head. Do you often get trapped in bad weather out here?" Holding my breath, I'm hoping he will take the bait on the subject change, and thankfully, he does.

"At least once a year. It's not uncommon when you're on long hunting trips to not make it back before the weather hits."

We finish lunch and begin the trek back home.

"It sounds like you and your dad were really close," he says.

"Yeah, it's always just been him and me. We took care of each other, and he was always my biggest cheerleader. What about your parents?"

"We were pretty close, but they're no longer around."

I don't miss the short and vague answer, but I want to use this time to try to get to know him a little more.

"Is that why you moved out here to the mountain?"

"Partly." While his tone is friendly, it's also vague, and if the short answers are any indication, he really doesn't want to talk about this. Deciding to let it go, as it wouldn't be fair for me to press an issue with him when I'm not willing to talk about things myself. When I don't press, he seems relieved, and we talk about some of our favorite camping moments with our families.

He's definitely easy to talk to, and we have a lot of the same interests. I find myself smiling quite a bit, and it's all about stuff I wasn't expecting.

My expectations were more along the line that I'd be with some guy that I could barely stand, and if I were lucky, would ignore me until it was time to talk about having kids. I wasn't expecting to actually like my husband or for him to be this handsome man and be such a good person. I had assumed that the only guys that would do the mail-order bride thing couldn't get a wife in real life, so they had to resort to getting one via the website. I've never been happier to be wrong.

The problem is the more I like him, the worse I feel about keeping a secret from him. It would be better if he weren't a good guy, then I wouldn't feel so bad about keeping all this to myself. But the nicer he is and the closer we get, the more I want to tell him. I can't take that chance just yet.

Chapter 6

Bennett

Today, I'm taking Willow into town. We have a few things to do, but she seems a little uncomfortable and on edge. When I told her about the cave, I picked up on something yesterday out by the lake. I wanted her to know there is a safe place for her if she ever needs it. But she got real quiet afterward, and I think she's beginning to wonder if I know something or suspect something, but neither of us has brought it up. While I have no intention of bringing it up unless she does, the last thing I need is for her to think that she can't trust me or she gets too uncomfortable and decides not to stay. If she's not here, I can't help protect her.

I park my truck behind Jack's shop because I know he won't mind. Then we walk down Main

Street stopping at a few stores before she finds a dress she really likes for Cash's wedding. As she casually takes in the town, we visit a few other shops.

When she doesn't think I'm looking, I notice how she's hyperaware of her surroundings, which only confirms my suspicions that she's worried about something.

Our last stop for the day is to see Jack. I have a box of things for him in the back of my truck. Mostly some bows and arrows that I've made for hunting. The tourists seemed to eat that kind of stuff up when they visit. So long as they keep buying, I'll keep making them.

After I finish unloading the stuff from my truck, I see she's talking to Jack with a big smile on her face.

"You really think my quilts would do well here?" she asks.

Jack gives me a nod, acknowledging that I'm with them now.

"Local handcrafted stuff does pretty well. I don't see why a quilt wouldn't either. You could bring one in, and we could put it up and test it and see how it goes."

"Oh, that would be great." Then her smile drops, and she looks over at me, "as long as that's okay with you."

"Sweetheart, if that's what you want to do, you're more than welcome to do it."

That seems to stun her for just a moment before she breaks into a huge smile.

"Just in case proper introductions were not done, Jack here owns the store." Then I look at Jack, "this is Willow, my soon-to-be wife." Willow's eyes go wide when I introduce her that way. She may still have the choice to leave, but as far as I'm concerned, she's going to be my wife. Even though Jack was here when I made the announcement that I had found my wife, he still looks a little shocked. Maybe he, much like my friends, didn't believe me when I originally said it.

"Jack here used to be a lawyer before he opened the shop. He still practices but only takes on cases that he chooses. Though he's worked with all of us that live up on the mountain with different things from contracts to probate."

"I also volunteer down at the local women's shelter a few towns over," Jack says. "When I was practicing law, I had to defend whatever case the practice gave me, even if they were guilty of some horrific crime. It was my job to get them acquitted, and I didn't enjoy getting the guilty off. So, I came down to Whiskey River for a weekend away to clear my head, and the shop was for sale. Before I went home, I had bought it, and now I just take on cases where I know I'm truly helping someone and not helping the bad guy."

Willow gives a polite smile but doesn't say much, but I hope she understands that I plan to surround her with people who can help her with whatever her problem might be. In time, maybe she'll trust me enough to tell me what has her frightened. If she doesn't reach out to me, hopefully, she'll tell someone who can help her.

But I want her to know that there are plenty of ways that I can protect her, and I plan to do just that. She doesn't say much afterward, but I'm assuming she's just processing everything that was said. I'm not going to push her for an answer she's not ready to give. So, I'm already trying to find a safe topic for the drive home as we go out to the car.

But once in the parking lot, she surprises me.

"Jack seems like a nice guy, but the only experience I've ever had with lawyers is how they manipulate the system."

It's not much to go on, but it is an insight into what is going on in her life.

"Some for sure do. Maybe more than many people realize, but Jack isn't one of them," I say. "He is one of the good guys and damn good at what he does. I wouldn't even bring you around him if he wasn't. He's at a point now where he only helps people that truly need it, people that have been wronged or need help fighting against those crooked lawyers. They're the ones that keep trying to manipulate. "

She nods her head and turns to look out the window. A million things run through my head. Has she been accused of something that she hasn't done? Is someone chasing after her, or is she hiding?

For a brief moment, I think of contacting a friend down at the police station and having him look into her. Then I decide that if I want her to trust me, I have to give her the same trust, which means waiting until she wants to talk.

Chapter 7

Willow

Today, we're camping at the lake, and Bennett insists on setting up the camping area himself. He tells me that it's his job to take care of me. I started to get a little nervous when I realized he only had one tent. Of course, Bennett being Bennett picked up on this right away.

"There's plenty of room inside this tent for both of us, but I'd rather have you close because we are out in the wild. Though I will promise you that there will be no sex until we are married. I won't push for it."

I know he's a man of his word, and for some reason, that little admission and promise were enough to make me relax. Also, I don't want to be alone out here either, even though I feel safer here than even at the house, and for the most part, I feel pretty safe at the house. Here on the mountain, it feels like no one can find me, and that feeling of freedom has allowed me to really relax.

"But Willow?" he says, getting my attention again.

"Just to be clear, I do want to marry you. All you have to do is say the word."

The look in his eyes is so intense there's no doubt he truly understands and means what he's saying.

I don't know what else to say, which seems to be a common occurrence around him. Once again, I just nod. He's leaving the choice up to me, so I want to take our camping trip here to get to know him, relax, and have fun.

Once the tent is set up and we've had lunch, we decide to swim in the lake. I go to the tent to change into my bathing suit. It isn't anything overly sexy; it's a one-piece. I'm pretty modest, especially by today's standards, yet when I step out of the tent in nothing but my bathing suit, time seems to stop. The look of pure heat and appreciation on his face is one every girl wants to see.

His eyes run over me, and there is no hiding the bulge in his jeans. I'm glad he likes what he sees because the feeling is completely mutual. When he finally pulls his eyes away from me, he clears his throat, and I make my way over to the lake.

Sticking my toes in the water, I gasp at how cold it is. But my body quickly adjusts, and just like my dad taught me, I dive in headfirst. Once I get the shock of the initial coldness out of the way, I resurface and turn toward Bennett. He's already waist-deep in the water and heading toward me.

He doesn't slow down until he's right in front of me and scoops me up out of the water and into his arms. Then he continues to walk deeper into the lake to the point where I wouldn't be able to stand up.

"Thank God you didn't step out of there in a bikini. If you look this hot in just a one-piece, I can't imagine how crazy you would drive me in a bikini," he says as his lips dance across my neck.

I tilt my head back to give him more access. Feeling him like this with as much skin as we have touching feels amazing. My nipples are hard and brushing against his chest, sending shivers and goosebumps racing across my skin.

His lips glide across mine. I can tell he's holding back with this kiss, and I'm holding back too. Seeing Bennett without his shirt and his washboard abs and that cut line pointing to interesting stuff almost make me forget all the reasons why I should be keeping him at arm's length. Not that I've had a very good success rate of being able to do so when his touch and his kiss feel like this.

My thighs cradle his hard cock and the tip rests against my clit, driving me crazy with each step he takes further into the water.

"Bennett," I moan. Not sure if it's a plea to stop or to keep going.

But he understands and puts space between us before diving under the water to cool off.

We spend the next half hour in the lake splashing around, playing, and having a good time. I can't remember the last time I laughed so hard, but I know it was long before my dad died or even got sick.

Once we get out and dry off, we decide to go on a short hike around the lake. He hands me a water bottle and takes one for himself before we head off on a slightly overgrown trail.

It's fairly flat around the lake, so it's an easy walk. But if you were to walk closer to the shore, you'd be walking on the rocks, and there would be no footprints. I make a note of that on the off chance I ever have to use this place.

"The lake has some good fishing, and there's a net in the cave as well." He tells me as we continue along the trail.

Getting to the side of the lake with the cave, I notice it's a little cooler because of the shade. But when we enter the cave, it's pretty much exactly as he described. Looking around, I see it's a great place to get out of the weather, with a small place to start a fire if needed. There are some bins with blankets, clothes, and food. Against one wall is a little makeshift bed and against the other is a stack of dry wood.

As we walk back to the campsite, we take a path around the opposite side, much like the other one. Only it just seems to take a bit longer to get back to the camp.

"Well, I thought I was going to keep my mouth shut about this, but I'm going to say this just so that it's out there and it's never a question in your mind. I know you're running from something, and I don't care what it is. I will protect you. You don't have to tell me what it is until you're ready, if ever. But for now, me and the other guys here will keep you safe."

With that, he takes my hand, and we continue back to the campsite. All I can think about is how the hell did I get so lucky. This could have gone a completely different way.

Once there, we take some time to relax. While he fishes in the lake, I lay there on a blanket and read. It's nice being in each other's company and enjoying our time together. It's the first time we are both truly at ease and being ourselves.

I'm not anxious until it's time to go to bed in the tent that we are going to share. Bennett must sense my nervousness because he takes my hand.

"I meant what I said, Willow. We'll wait till our wedding night. For now, I just want you to relax and be comfortable around me."

Slipping inside the tent, I see he's placed our sleeping bags on completely opposite sides of the tent. It doesn't give us much room, but just the thought that he was trying to give me as much space as possible calms me.

But Bennett is a big man, and I don't want him cramped either. So before he can lie down, I pull his sleeping bag closer to mine. Though he watches me, he doesn't say anything. Once we crawl into our sleeping bags and we're facing each other, he reaches out and takes my hand in his.

"You aren't what I was expecting when I signed up to do this," I tell him honestly.

"You're not what I expected when I started looking at those online dating profiles either. But I'm really glad I found you."

He says that now and he says he'll protect me no matter what, but I have to wonder if he knew the whole story if he really would. But I can't worry about that now. Instead, for the time being, I'm just going to let it be and enjoy the safety of being out here in the middle of nowhere.

It's like he knows the thoughts running around in my head and wants to silence them. He cups the back of my head and drags me slowly towards him until his lips land on mine. Like magnets, our bodies are pulled together by an invisible force until there is no space left between us.

He opens his sleeping bag and pulls me into it. The cold night air was a shock to my system, but he closes the sleeping bag around us, and his warmth and his scent surround me. Keeping me safe.

How can one person feel at home in such a short period of time?

His lips crush mine as he deepens the kiss and his tongue dances with mine, and I can feel every stroke of it all over my body. One of his rough hands holds me close while the other angles my head so he can kiss down my neck.

His hot breath races across my skin and his lips place the softest kisses on my neck. The combination had my skin breaking out in goosebumps, my nipples hard, and my panties soaked.

"Bennett," I whisper because it's almost too much.

I want more, more than I can give right now, but at the same time, I don't want him to stop. He pulls back from our embrace and places a kiss on my forehead before tucking my head under his chin.

"Get some sleep, sweetheart. I'll be right here the whole time."

Chapter 8

Bennett

Even though I've always loved camping, I can't remember having a better time on a camping trip than I did these past few days with Willow. It wasn't just that I got to hold her and kiss her at night. Because that was amazing too, mainly, it was how much we connected and how comfortable it was being with her. When I finally admitted to her that I knew she was running from something, but I didn't care, she finally let down her guard and seemed to relax and trust me. Hopefully, soon she'll trust me with the story of what is going on, but until then, I can be patient. Well, at least for now.

Today is Cash's wedding, and she's in our room getting dressed. I can't wait to see her in the dress she picked out, and I'm excited to show her off even though it's to friends and only up here on the mountain.

When she steps out of our room, she looks absolutely stunning in the dark blue dress that hugs every curve.

"Are you sure about these shoes?" she asks me.

She wanted to wear heels to go with the dress, but it's an outside wedding on the mountain, so I was able to convince her to wear flats.

"I promise you're going to want to be in the flats. Your feet will be so much more comfortable." I try to reassure her.

Taking her hand, we head out to my truck. It's just a short drive there, but I can tell she's a bit anxious.

"They already love you. There is no reason to be nervous." I take her hand, bring it to my lips, and place a soft kiss.

Jana and Cole will be getting married in two weeks, and she agreed to go to their wedding with me as well. But I get the feeling she's thinking about the fact that sometime between there will be our wedding.

While I want to give her a huge one, I also want her tied to me as soon as possible. Three weddings in three weeks on the mountain. Who would have ever thought? Certainly not any of us.

The wedding is being held outside at Cash's house. It's just a very simple wedding with only their closest friends because they don't have any family.

After the wedding, everyone mingles. The girls form one group, and the men stick to the other. As I'm talking, I feel her eyes on me, and every time I look up she's smiling at me or she'll give me a cute little wink. She's very flirtatious today, and I hope that means that she's more comfortable with me.

"She seems a lot more relaxed today," Phoenix says as he catches me watching her.

"I agree. We went camping and had time to talk and take it easy, which seemed to help quite a bit," I admit.

"That's what worked for us, too." Cash has a smile on his face as he watches his new bride.

For about an hour, we all stay, talking and snacking. Finally, Hope and Cash kick us out so they can properly celebrate their wedding night.

During the ride home, Willow holds my hand and tells me what the girls talked about after the wedding. If it meant just hearing the sound of her voice, I could listen to her talk about anything.

Once we're home and inside, she gets shy, like she wants to say something but isn't sure.

"What is it, sweetheart?" I pull her into me.

"It's just... when we were camping, I got really used to you sleeping beside me. Will you sleep in bed with me tonight?"

I groan because that sounds like the sweetest torture I can imagine, but I can also read between the lines. She felt safe with me there, and if that's what she needs, then I will give it to her even if it means the worst case of blue balls I've ever had.

"Of course I will. Now go get ready for bed."

As she gets ready, I walk around the house and do a security check, making sure all the doors and windows are locked and that nothing is out of place. She trusts me to keep her safe, and I won't break that trust.

Once she crawls into bed, I go to the bathroom and take a few minutes to calm myself. Because the last thing she wants is for me to jump her the moment I get into bed.

She wastes no time snuggling right up to my side when I get into bed with her. I love the fact that she's comfortable with me because I absolutely love having her in my arms.

"So, I was thinking," she says, and my whole body tenses because this could go either way.

She rubs her hand over my chest as if she's trying to relax me before she continues.

"I think we should get married. Just a small, simple courthouse wedding next weekend. Something your friends can attend as we don't really have a family to invite."

My heart literally skips a beat because I want nothing more than to make her my wife. But I want to make sure she's doing it for her and for the right reasons.

"Why the change of heart?"

"Because I want many more nights like this. And I want more camping trips too. If you can make me feel this safe after only a couple of weeks, I can't wait to spend the next couple of years together."

"I can't wait either. So next weekend sounds perfect. You worry about the dress, and I'll make sure everything else is taken care of." At my words, a huge smile crosses her face.

We lay there as she gently traces her hand up and down my chest. Every movement turns me on a little more. I don't even try to hide how hard she makes me.

I know the moment she sees my cock tenting my pants because her breath catching in the sexiest, quiet gasp. What I don't expect is for her to reach down and grip my cock.

It feels so good I groan out loud. For so many years, my cock has not felt anything but my own hand. She strokes me a few times, and I'm already so close to the edge, but I can't let that happen.

In the blink of an eye, I flip us, so I'm on top of her, caging her in and pinning her wrists above her head.

"You are first," I tell her and reach one hand into her panties to find her already wet and waiting for me.

Using her juices to coat my fingers, I play with her clit. The moan she gives as she arches her back is almost my undoing. Letting her hands go, I hold myself above her while I continue to finger her.

She wastes no time reaching into my pants for my cock, and this time I don't stop her. I watch how she reacts to every stroke of her clit because I need to know how to drive her as crazy as she makes me feel.

My movements get more frantic the closer she gets to making me cum all over her stomach. As her orgasm takes over, she doesn't stop stoking me. Just watching her cum is hot enough that I couldn't stop mine if I tried.

I watch stream after stream of warm white cum coat her panties and up her stomach, and I think the only thing that would look sexier is my ring on her finger while I was doing it.

Chapter 9

Willow

Today, after the wedding, we are taking a lazy day. Both of us are working inside, me on the t-shirt quilt I'm making and him on a set of bows and arrows. I love watching him work with his hands. He knows what he's doing, and his movements are easy and sure.

As much as I enjoy watching him, he's also keeping a close eye on me. There is something so comforting about the normalcy of this moment. I hope we have many more days like this.

If this is what life is like up on the mountain, I'm really kicking myself for not doing something like this sooner. My dad would have loved this, but we were both so stuck in Chicago and our lives there. I wish he could have had a chance to experience a life like this before he died.

I can't remember the last time I slept as well as I did last night in Bennett's arms. He made me feel safe and protected. But at the same time, it makes me feel guilty for not sharing exactly what's going on in my life. Then I think about how well things are going and I don't want to burst the bubble. Not yet, anyway. While I know I will have to tell him eventually, I want to enjoy this time with him right now.

When I look up at him again, I find him already looking at me. He doesn't turn away but continues to let his eyes roam down my body. With his eyes on me, it's as if his hands are on my skin, caressing me.

While studying my every move, he says, "Every year, I do some trading with the local farmer whose property borders the edge of my property at the back. I need to go renegotiate this season's agreement. If I go up there this afternoon, do you want to go with me?"

He's waiting to see my reaction. I've noticed that he studies every little thing about me. It's as if he wants to know every detail or that I'm telling the truth about things. If I had to guess, I'd say he wants to make sure I'm not just saying yes to something to make him happy, or he wants to make sure that it's something I truly want.

"Yeah, I'd like to see you in action."

That earns me a smile from him, and we both finish up what we're doing and get ready to leave. Once in his car, I want to know more.

"So, what exactly is your agreement with them?"

"They use a part of my land strictly for hay and pay me a land rent fee. But instead of cash, we swap meat, so it's that much less I have to hunt on my own. Now that you're here, it will be a huge help, and later as we grow our family."

He says it's so casually I don't think he realizes that his thinking about us building our family together is so much further out in the future than I ever dreamed of looking. I turn my head to look out the window so he can't see the flush that has covered my face.

Soon we're heading out of the mountains and down into flat land, passing farm after farm.

"Is this still Whiskey River?" I ask, trying to get my bearings.

"Technically, yes. The mountains are on the north side of town, and the farmland is more towards the east. I've dealt with this family for many years. There are four brothers who work running the ranch, and then they have a sister who helps out here and there. But I mostly work with and talk to the older brother."

Finally, he turns down one of the long driveways, and we make our way up to a farmhouse. We're greeted by a barking dog running off the front porch to our car. Right behind the dog is an honest-to-God cowboy in wranglers and a cowboy hat coming outside to greet us.

"Bennett! We were just talking about you and hoping you'd stop by soon," the cowboy says as we step out of the truck. "And you brought a pretty lady with you."

"This is my fiancé, Willow. Willow, this is Jasper. He's the one that I was telling you about," Bennett introduces us.

"Why don't you come inside, and we'll talk," Jasper says as we follow him into the house.

After making sure that we don't want anything to eat or drink, he sits down in the recliner next to the couch, and he and Bennett start talking about their agreement.

Looking around, I check out the house, which seems to be what I would expect a typical ranch house to look like. But then I notice a woman standing in the doorway shooting daggers at me.

"Emma, why don't you come in and join us instead of hanging out by the door," Jasper says as the woman steps into the room.

"Willow, this is my sister Emma, and Emma, this is Bennett's fiancé, Willow," Jasper introduces us.

At the mention of the word fiancé, the look on her face couldn't get any more disgusted, but it's quickly gone when she glances over at Bennett. Then she attempts a flirtatious smile aimed at him.

I have to admit I get a certain satisfaction out of the fact that he completely ignores her. Instead, Bennett focuses on either Jasper or me, which appears to irritate her even more.

As her flirting attempts fail, she tries to take it out on me with what I'm assuming she thinks are scary looks. It does make me wonder what kind of history she and Bennett have.

"But did Jasper tell you about the new colt that we have? she interrupts. "I'd be happy to show it to you in the barn," she says while playing with her hair and pushing out her breasts. The fact that she doesn't even try to hide that she's flirting with him makes her look overly desperate, at least in my opinion. But maybe that's what Bennett likes. I don't know.

"No thanks, Emma. Maybe Willow would like to see it while we finish up our meeting." Bennett turns his smile to me, but I'm not stupid enough to take him up on that offer of going into the barn alone with Emma. That would pretty much be suicide.

"I'm good right here," I say with a smile and take Bennett's hand, which earns me another smile from him and another glare from Emma. As he talks to Jasper, he grips my hand and rubs his thumb over the back of my hand. It is not much longer before they wrap up their conversation.

"You ready to head home, sweetheart?" Bennett asks when they're done.

"I'm ready if you are."

We say our goodbyes, and as always, Bennett is a perfect gentleman, opening my truck door and making sure I'm inside before getting in himself. Once we're on the road and going toward home, I decide to ask the question that's been floating around in my head.

"What's the deal with you and Emma?" I ask bluntly.

"There's nothing there. She's more like the annoying little kid sister. When Jasper and I first started working together, she was always around, and I learned to ignore her. Why?"

He glances at me for a second before his eyes land back on the road.

"I was just wondering because she was trying awfully hard to get your attention the entire time we were there."

"Well, you completely had my attention and made it very hard for me to concentrate on Jasper. Actually, I didn't even notice her other than when she asked about the colt and the barn," he says, squeezing my hand.

"Well, that was a blatant attempt to get you away from me and alone with her." I don't know where this sassy part of me came from, feeling like I own him and have the right to be upset about the way that Emma acted. For all I know, they could have a history and one he isn't wanting to admit to having.

"Didn't I turn that down really quick? I understand with us moving so quickly, and women like her can give you pause, but you'll learn to trust me. At some point, you'll learn I'm a man of my word."

Deciding to give him the benefit of the doubt, I drop the subject. He deserves at least that, and besides, the truth always comes out one way or another.

Chapter 10

Bennett

Ever since we visited the ranch, Willow seems to have been off the past few days. Even though I can't put my finger on why, I do know one thing for sure, we're getting married tomorrow. There's absolutely no way I want her to have any doubts or cold feet. But at the same time, I want to marry her more than my next breath.

It would crush me if she decided she didn't want to get married, but I'm also not going to force her into this either. I don't want her to feel like she has to get married just to have protection from whatever it is she's running from. No matter what, I'll protect her.

Once again, we're in the living room. She's working on the quilt, and I'm making some arrows for the bow. Without giving it too much thought, I decide it's time to breach the subject.

"You aren't having cold feet, are you?" I ask.

Immediately, she stops dead and looks up at me. "No, are you?"

At least now I have her full attention.

"No, but you've just been off for the last few days. I want to make it very clear to you that you don't have to marry me. Whatever happens, even if you decide not to marry me, I will protect you."

The words feel like acid coming out of my mouth, but I know it's the right thing to do. She must be considering my words because she sits there, not moving or saying anything. Finally, she sets her quilt stuff down and walks over to me.

Her face looks so serious that I prepare myself for bad news. When she reaches me, I go to stand up, but she places a hand on my chest, stopping me, and then sits down in my lap, straddling me.

Her hands run through my hair and then down to the side of my face to angle my face up to hers.

"I want to marry you, and I will marry you." Without letting me respond, her lips are on mine, kissing me gently.

Even though I'm trying to do the right thing, it's just not possible when I have the taste of her on me.

When I wrap my arms around her waist and pull her into me, it feels right and perfect with her in my arms. As much as I hate it, I pull back after a moment.

"I want to marry you too, sweetheart. More than you know. But I don't want you to feel like you're being forced into this just because you need my help. You'll have that regardless." I'm hoping it sinks in.

"I know that, Bennett, I do. And I don't want to marry you just for protection. I really feel something between us. Maybe that's why I've been off. I absolutely hated it when Emma was flirting with you and trying to get your attention."

"You are the only girl that has my attention or will have my attention until my dying day. I can promise you that."

That earn me a huge smile, and she leans in for another soft kiss.

"Okay, sweetheart, you need to get back to work. We need to finish these projects." In reality, the last thing I want is for her to get off my lap.

She seems just as reluctant but stands and goes back over to work on her quilt. After our conversation, the old Willow is back. She's flirting and looking at me with sexy heat in her eyes. Maybe we just needed to clear the air. Whatever it was, I'm glad she's back.

The only problem is flirty Willow is damn hard to resist. She makes me so turned on, and I want nothing more than to take her here and now on the couch. But I made her promise that we'd wait till our wedding night, and I want her to know that she can always trust me and when I say something, it's the truth. I never want to give her a reason to doubt my word. So, we'll wait even if that means I continue to suffer with the worst case of blue balls ever.

Flirting doesn't stop one bit for the rest of the day, and thank God we are getting married tomorrow. After dinner, I can tell she's just as turned on as I am by the way she's rubbing her thighs together and the outline of her nipples under her shirt.

She's sitting in the living room trying to read a book, but she keeps biting her lip and rubbing her thighs together. Finally, I just can't take anymore.

I'm in front of her before she realizes it, pulling her leggings down and spreading her legs wide.

"Bennett!" she squeals.

"I can tell you're in need, and it's driving me crazy," I tell her, my voice more gruff than normal as I settle between her thighs.

She sets her book down and relaxes in the chair. My first taste of her proves she is as turned on as I thought she was. She is soaked and overly sensitive at even my slightest touch.

When she reaches up to play with my hair, I close my eyes and get lost in her. The sensations of her hands in my hair and her taste on my tongue send my body into overdrive.

I slide two fingers into her, and she gasps, followed by a groan before her entire body tenses up. I know she's close, but I pull back and look up at her. She opens her eyes.

"Why?" she asks breathlessly.

"Not ready for you to cum yet, sweetheart," I kiss just below her belly button before sucking her clit back into my mouth.

Instantly, her body is right back where it was, wanting release, and barely hanging on. Her hands are back in my hair and my cock is begging for attention. Using my free hand, I pull him out and start slowly stroking him.

I match my strokes to the strokes of my tongue on her clit, speeding up and pressing as my fingers thrust in and out of her. When she starts pulling my hair and screaming my name and her back arches off the chair, I finally let myself fall over the edge and spill my seed on the wood floor.

When I look back up at Willow, her eyes are closed, and she has a satisfied smile on her face. This will do for tonight, but tomorrow night I will finish inside her wet heat.

Chapter 11

Willow

Today is my wedding day.

I'm excited to marry Bennett, but a small part of me has been dreading today, too. My dad isn't here to walk me down the aisle. He isn't here to give Bennett his blessing. Of course, if my dad was here, I never would have met Bennett, so there is that.

In the end, we decided to have a small, simple courthouse wedding. Nothing even half as fancy as what Cash and Hope had, even though theirs was very casual as well. Jana and Cole are having a wedding much like Hope and Cash.

Even though it's a small simple wedding, all the couples are here. The girls have helped me get ready, even sharing some of their makeup since I didn't have any.

I found a vintage lace dress at the thrift store in town that's serving as my wedding dress. After having an argument about why I was kicking Bennett out of the house for a few hours the other day, I was able to alter it slightly to fit me. Though he didn't venture far. The entire time, he was outside doing chores right around the house. I may not have said it to him, but I'm glad that he stayed really close.

I may feel protected on the mountain, but I feel even safer when he's around. Something about him, especially at night in his arms, it's like nothing can touch me.

"Okay. Your hair has the perfect curls in it, so now we just need to hairspray the shit out of it," Jana says, and the other girls start giggling.

Jack has been nice enough to allow us to use a room in his shop to get ready. He even promised Bennett, who was waiting at the courthouse, that Axel and he would walk us over to the courthouse. That way, all of us ladies would not be alone. The rest of the guys are with Bennett at the courthouse. But I can only imagine how much he hates being away from me because I'm really hating being away from him, too.

A moment later, the room erupts in a huge cloud of hairspray.

"There, that should hold your hair for at least a few hours," Jana says.

"Look at me," Emelie says. When I turn my head to the left to look at her, she does a quick makeup check before applying my lipstick and lip gloss.

"You ready, little one?" Axel peeks his head in to check on us. Not once since we got here has he left the doorway.

"Are you ready, Willow?" Emelie asks, and when I nod, everyone grabs their stuff and we head out.

The walk to the courthouse is not far. It's just across the street and a few buildings down from Jack's shop. But the walk seems to take forever.

Maybe it's because I know Bennett is inside, or maybe it's because I'm trying to remember this moment. Someday I might want to look back and remember exactly what I felt.

As we walk, I'm enjoying the weather. It's nice and calm, almost quiet. The serenity along with the fresh mountain air and the sun on my face feels amazing, but the moment we step into the courthouse, it's like full-on chaos. There's noise and people moving all around, and I'm ushered right to the room where we're having the wedding ceremony.

I go through all the motions and before I know it, I'm standing at the end of the aisle with Bennett staring back at me. Both of us have huge smiles on our faces. He's made it very clear how much he wants this, and he doesn't even try to hide it amongst his friends.

Standing here on our wedding day, he's looking at me just like every bride hopes their groom would look at them. In that instant, a very small part of me wishes we had done the big traditional wedding with the long walk down the aisle, so I could soak up that look even more. But then I know I wouldn't have wanted to wait to get married, so this is perfect for us.

The officiant keeps the wedding short, sweet, and to the point. Once we say our vows, in the blink of an eye, he's kissing me as we are pronounced husband and wife.

Bennett has always been a good kisser, but this kiss just feels different. Maybe it's because he's officially my husband, or maybe it's because this is a kiss with everyone watching, but it's definitely a hell of a lot sexier than any kiss before it.

While I don't know how long he kisses me, eventually his friends start whistling and the girls are giggling. Only then do we pull apart and turn to face everyone. My face feels like it's on fire and I bet I'm as red as a tomato, but everyone else is smiling and cheering.

Jana, who used to manage the cafe was able to pull some strings and got us a spot to have a small wedding reception and lunch before we all go back up the mountain.

Once all the paperwork is completed at the courthouse, we meet everybody at the cafe, and have a great afternoon with our friends talking and laughing. Though it isn't a fancy wedding reception with a DJ, a catered meal, and dancing, I don't think I could imagine anything more perfect. I can't remember the last time I laughed this hard. It's been a long time, but this is exactly the day that I needed to have for my wedding day.

Finally, everyone starts saying their goodbyes and leaving. Bennett tells me we have a little bit of a drive because he's booked us a hotel a few towns over for a little honeymoon, as he calls it. When Bennett says he hasn't spent a night off the mountain in over six years, I know this is a big deal for him. Not only does it mean a lot that he's so thoughtful, but I'm touched as well. It will make another nice memory for our honeymoon weekend.

Bennett's truck is parked in Jack's parking lot, so we walk hand-in-hand down the street. Before we get there, we run into the last person I expected to see today. Emma.

"Bennett! Wow, this is an unexpected surprise. I've never run into you in town before."

It makes me gag how her voice is so flirty and sweet.

Almost like Bennett can read my mind, the hand that's holding mine tightens like he's afraid I'm going to try to run off. Though he's not wrong, I'd rather leave than stand here and deal with her. But it doesn't look like Bennett's going to allow me to escape.

"Emma," he nods, barely acknowledging her before trying to walk away.

But of course, she's not going to let it go that easily.

"What are you doing in town? Usually you just go to Jack's shop."

She's trying to keep any thread of the conversation going, but once again Bennett squeezes my hand and I'm starting to wonder whose comfort he's doing it for, mine or his.

"We are in town today because Willow and I got married. Now if you will excuse us, we have a honeymoon to go to."

That seems to shock her and stop her in her tracks. When he tries to walk around her, she doesn't move. I would take joy in the pure shock on her face if it wasn't for a second later the ugly look on her face when she glares at me. Not only is it with hatred, but with derision like she's not quite sure what I did to deserve Bennett. I'm used to girls being petty, which is why Aspen was really my only friend who was a girl.

Briefly, I wonder how Aspen's doing. I know she decided to go the virgin auction route at Club Red in Chicago. Since the auction is in a few days, hopefully, I'll be able to hear from her soon. For a moment, I consider having Bennett stop at Jack's so that I can send her an email.

"I can't wait to get you alone and not have to share your attention," Bennett says once we hit the parking lot.

Any thought of trying to delay our small little honeymoon is gone, and anticipation takes its place.

The ride to the hotel seems to take forever, even though in reality it's only forty minutes. When we pull up to the hotel, he goes to check us in and then comes back to get me and the bags.

I was expecting some simple little hotel, but he totally surprised me. This hotel is grand, definitely upscale. He picked one of the fanciest ones in town, and I'm thrilled with his thoughtfulness. Even though the hotel isn't that tall with only five floors, with us being on the fifth floor, we'll probably have a fantastic view.

And I certainly wasn't expecting him to have booked the actual honeymoon suite, or for him to carry me over the threshold. The room is lit by candlelight with rose petals on the floor and the bed. It's like something out of a fairy tale.

"You did this?" I ask, looking at all the small details around the room.

"I wanted you to have an amazing wedding. While it may have just been at the courthouse with some of our friends and a honeymoon at a hotel a few towns over, I wanted it to be as special as it could be," he says.

When I turn around, his eyes are on me.

"This is absolutely perfect," I tell him as a huge smile crosses his face.

Was he really worried that I wouldn't like it? How could any girl not like this? It's the romantic gesture that every woman wants in her relationship, and something I absolutely would not have expected from a mountain man like Bennett.

"Let me help you out of that dress." He takes a few steps toward me.

Turning my back to him, I pull my hair to the side to reveal the buttons and zipper. I hear his footsteps and when he steps behind me, his body heat engulfs my back. He traces a hand down the side of my neck, making me shiver at the feel of his hands.

As he slowly unbuttons the three buttons at the top, he takes his time, making it clear he's in no rush. When he reaches the top of the zipper, he stops and leans down to place a few soft kisses on the base of my neck. Once again, they send chills up my body.

Then he ever so slowly pulls the zipper down, kissing my exposed skin. He's taking his time and driving me crazy. I want to rush things along, but at the same time, I don't want it to end. All these different feelings are bombarding me. I want more, but he's in no rush.

It seems like hours before my dress finally hits the floor. The second it does, I'm spinning around, wrapping my arms around him and pulling him in for a kiss, pressing every inch of my body to his. He works at unhooking my bra and it falls to the ground as I stand there in only my thin panties.

His hands grip my ass before lifting me up and placing me on the bed ever so gently. At last, he's finally taking off his clothes, and I'm enjoying the show. When he notices me watching, he slows down and puts on a little striptease for me.

Every inch of his skin that's revealed sets my skin on fire. I'm soaked between my thighs, and I want him more than I ever thought possible. For the first time, I get to see him completely naked and it's hard to breathe. He's got muscles that I didn't even know existed. Tattoos and scars cover his skin, but they only make him sexier.

Stepping forward, he takes my underwear off and steps between my legs. Then he pulls my ass to the edge of the bed, which happens to be the perfect height for him. As we stare at each other on full display and completely naked, we're both breathing hard.

With only his eyes on me, it feels like his hands are roaming over my body. I feel every movement.

After a minute, he moves his hands up and down my body, stopping at my breasts to lick my hard nipples. Then he moves down to my pussy and plays with my clit, making me writhe. At the same time, his cock nuzzles my entrance.

Our eyes lock and he stokes my clit more before slowly pressing into me. The slow stretch feels so damn good that we both groan. He's gentle with me, taking his time. I expected him to be a little rougher with all the teasing and waiting we have been doing. But no, he is still unhurried.

With slow, shallow thrusts, he moves in and out of me until he is seated all the way in me.

"Look how well my wife takes my cock. Fuck, it's the most beautiful sight I've ever seen in my life." He moans as he picks up the pace.

He continues stroking my clit and keeping me on edge. Each thrust is a bit harder and more powerful, causing my breasts to bounce. If he wasn't holding me in place, I know I'd be halfway off the bed by now.

The heat in his eyes alone has me turned on. But every sensation and every thrust heightens until every muscle in my body locks up and the world around me seems to freeze in time as my orgasm crashes into me.

Only when my husband collapses on top of me do I regain consciousness. I can feel his warm release dripping from me. Before I can think about moving, he goes to the bathroom and returns with a warm cloth, carefully cleaning me up before situating me in bed.

I've never had someone take such good care of me. It's just proves these mountain men are a different breed.

Chapter 12

Bennett

I don't think I could imagine a more perfect morning than waking up and having my wife in my arms. Last night was amazing, but as I sit here and hold Willow, watching her sleep, I know that this is how I want every day to start.

In her sleep, she looks so peaceful and innocent. Just looking at her makes me hard as hell, but after last night, she has to be sore. So, as much as I'd like to wake her up and take her again, I'm going to give her a break.

Instead, I lie here, and I watch her sleep. The light peeking through the curtains hits off her hair and it gleams in the sunlight. There's a hint of a smile on her face, and God, I hope she's dreaming of me.

Since I have no intention of waking her up, I continue to lie here and enjoy the sight of my beautiful wife. I memorize every curve of her face, the way her eyelashes rest against her cheek, how her hair gently falls onto her face, and the slight flush of her skin.

Lying there, she looks like an angel, and it is absolutely the most wonderful thing I've ever seen. I don't know how long I lay here, but once she starts stirring, I slowly climb out of bed and order room service for us. Then I climb back into bed and place a soft kiss on her forehead.

That's when she wakes up and looks at me with a soft smile just for me. When she stretches, it causes the blanket to dip down just enough that her perfect and perky tits are on full display. The temptation is so great that I lean down and suck on the nipple closest to me just enough for it to harden in my mouth, before I turn and do the same to the other one.

She wraps her arms around my neck and tries to pull me in for more.

"Not this morning, sweetheart. I know you're sore, and I just ordered room service. Let's get out of the hotel for a while today and then we'll come back and take a nice warm bath together."

One of the best things about this honeymoon suite is there's a jacuzzi tub in the room and it's plenty big enough for both of us.

"That sounds perfect."

"Hurry and get dressed before the food gets here." I playfully push her towards the end of the bed and give her ass a good smack as she gets up and makes her way to the bathroom.

Thankfully, she's in there when room service gets here, so I don't have to worry about them seeing her. They're gone before she steps back out in nothing but one of my t-shirts. Even though it is sexy as hell, I would have been pissed if the room service guy had seen her like this.

When she gives me a wink before she sits down at the little table where we set up the food, I know she knows how I was feeling.

Not sure what she would be in the mood for today, I ordered several of her favorite foods figuring that whatever she doesn't eat, I will. She looks at the bounty before her and smiles while grabbing the huckleberry French toast and a bowl of fruit, digging in.

"I didn't realize how hungry I was," she says after the first few bites.

"Well, we really worked up at appetite last night and I plan to do it again tonight." This time it's me throwing a wink at her, and the flush that crosses her face is absolutely stunning.

We finish up breakfast and take a little longer than normal to get ready and head out for the day.

Our hotel is right downtown, so we don't really have a plan. Walking hand-in-hand, we check out different shops and stop for whatever catches her eye. At the home decor shop, she picks out some pieces. But when she spots the fabric shop, we enter to find an array of fabric, sewing, and quilting supplies.

"Why don't you get whatever you want to make a few quilts? Once we get back in Whiskey River, you can place an order for fabric with Jack. But for now, get enough stuff to make two or three of them." I tell her as she eyes the fabric, and turns to face me with wide eyes.

"Really?" she asks almost in shock.

"Yes, sweetheart. Get whatever you want."

Giggling, she claps her hands and hurries over to go through the different fabrics. She pulls a blue fabric from the shelf and then holds it up next to a different blue fabric before pulling it from the shelf and handing them both to me. She repeats this process several more times with a different assortment until we finally go to a table. It's there the clerk cuts the fabric, wraps it up and we check out.

"What do you think about eating at that little Italian cafe we passed near the hotel?" I ask as we start making our way back.

I've had the image of her in the bathtub with me all morning, but I do want to make sure she at least has lunch before I make her forget her own name.

"That sounds perfect."

Maybe it's because she's teasing me, rubbing her foot up and down my leg and flirting the whole time, she seems to take forever to eat. She knows what she's doing to me. There's no point in trying to hide it from her because she can easily feel it.

· · · · • · • • · · ·

Willow

Our honeymoon weekend went by quickly and now we've been home for a few days, and everything is going really well. We've fallen into a great routine, one where he wakes me up with an orgasm every morning. Then while he takes a shower, I make breakfast. After that, we do our morning chores. While he does the work outside, I do the inside things like preparing dinner, laundry, and any other odds and ends I had planned.

When I've completed everything that had to be done, I sit down and I quilt. Once Bennett finishes whatever he has to do outside, he joins me inside to do some work.

Next week, we have plans to do some hunting. Just getting out of the house for the day will be nice. I'm really looking forward to it and having an opportunity to see more of his land.

While I finish up the dishes from breakfast, I'm enjoying staring at Bennett doing some work in the barn. I love this kitchen window, which gives me a great view of him and any work that he has to do out at the back of the house. My time watching him is interrupted by a knock at the door.

We aren't expecting anyone and I wonder if it's one of his friends needing something. Before opening the door, I check to see who is out there. I'm shocked to see Emma, of all people. Part of me wants to ignore her and not open the door, but it could be something important for one of her brothers. So, I paste on a fixed smile and open the door.

"Hello Emma, what can I do for you?" I say in as friendly of a voice as possible, but she stands there and just stares at me for a moment.

"I'm here to see Bennett," she says her voice cold.

"Well, he is out doing a few things around the property, but I'm happy to relay a message." Then I offer her another fake smile, which she has to know is not real.

She glares at me and says, "No, you can't. Just let him know that I'm here and I'll be down at the ranch when he's ready for me. You know him and I had a great thing going on before you showed up, and I'm not quite sure why he decided to marry you."

My protective instincts kick in hard and fast, especially after the weekend that we shared together.

"Bennett is the kind of man to do what he wants and if he wanted you, he'd be with you.

So obviously he's made his choice, and it's not you. Now you're just embarrassing yourself." I refrain from rolling my eyes, but boy, do I want to.

When Emma gets this evil smile on her face, I obviously have not made my point.

"You know, I'm sure he had his reasons for marrying you. Probably had to be pity. Because I know it's so pathetic watching you follow him around." Without another word, she turns around and gets into her car.

I'm fuming mad and now have so many comebacks that I wish I had thought of at the time.

When I go to the kitchen to finish drying and putting away the dishes, Bennett is nowhere to be seen. He's probably inside the barn. But Emma's words keep running through my head over and over and over again.

Since I'm hiding something from him, why wouldn't he hide something from me? After all, we haven't been completely honest with each other. While he's allowed it and hasn't pushed me, is it because if he pushed me to give him my secrets, he'd have to share his? That would be fair, wouldn't it? So, it makes sense. He doesn't push for my secrets, so he doesn't have to reveal his.

What if Emma is right? What if he did marry me because he felt sorry for me, knowing that I needed someone's help and protection? What if he just did it out of some sense of duty to keep me safe while getting laid at the same time?

Though that just doesn't seem like the Bennett I know. While he's outside, for another hour or so, I just continue to stew about what Emma said. My thoughts keep coming back around to I'm hiding something from him, so obviously, it wouldn't be a far stretch that he would be hiding something from me.

By the time he comes back inside, I'm irritated and annoyed and determined to get to the bottom of this. Because I will not have Emma on the outskirts of our relationship or what little of one there is at the moment.

"Whatever you have going for dinner smells amazing." He walks in oblivious to my mood, and gives me a kiss on the forehead.

"What's wrong, sweetheart?" he asks as he takes a step back, instantly concerned.

"What arrangement did you and Emma have?" I ask not even trying to hide the irritation in my voice.

"What? Where is this coming from? I told you that we never had anything between us. I look at her as more of a little sister."

"Really? Because she was over here earlier asking to talk to you. She wanted me to tell you that she'll be at the ranch whenever you're ready for her. Oh, and she also said you two had such a great thing going on before I got in the way."

"She was here?" he asks. Anger is all over his face, and I just nod.

"Damn it. She's never once been to my cabin. I didn't even know that she knew where it was." He runs a hand over his face and sighs.

It's easy to tell he's irritated. But is he annoyed because I finally called him out on it? I'm not sure.

"None of that is true, Willow. I've never once touched her, not even for a casual hug. There's nothing going on between us and there never has been."

Even though he seems sincere, I'm still not completely sure. Maybe it's because of my own doubt and my own secrets, or maybe it's just how convincing Emma was. I'm still uncertain.

"Let me prove it to you," he says, taking my hand.

While I'm not quite sure what he has in mind, but if he thinks he can prove it, then I'm going to let him.

Hesitantly, I place my hand in his.

"Okay. Prove it."

Chapter 13

Bennett

I'm still fuming that Emma had the audacity to step foot on my property. Much less to say any of that stuff to my wife. I will not have Willow doubting me and I'm angry Emma planted that seed of doubt. I could see it in Willow's eyes that Emma got under her skin and I'm not all right with it.

The only way I can prove it to her is to take her to their ranch. So, that's exactly what I'm doing.

When we arrive, I barely get out of the truck before Emma is stepping out onto the porch. A satisfied smirk covers her face, but it drops the moment she sees Willow get out of the truck. Willow looks pissed, and I can read that look on her face because it's clear as day. It says, why the fuck did you bring me here?

"Emma, now that we're both present, why don't you tell me exactly what you told Willow?" I don't even try to soften my tone. There's no point because anytime I'm nice to her, she takes it and runs a mile with it.

Before she even gets a chance to respond, Jasper and one of his younger brothers step out onto the porch. He clearly heard what I said and is staring at his sister waiting for her answer.

"I just told her the truth. She got in the way of what we had going on and that you married her out of pity." Then she rolls her eyes like it's the most normal thing in the world.

"Are you kidding me, Emma? We all know that he's never once touched you and there's been nothing going on. He's been more than gracious trying to put you off every time that he's here. Now it makes sense why you never leave the house when you know he's coming over. No matter how much we try. But going to his house and causing problems with his wife? You've got to be shitting me," Jasper says as he walks toward Willow.

"I don't know what game my sister is playing at, but you can ask any one of us and anyone in town. She and Bennett never had anything going on. When Bennett's been here, she's tried to flirt. We've seen it and we've told her to stop. But you need to know he puts her off every time. I'm so damned sorry for the trouble that she caused today."

Then he looks over at me. "I can't even express how sorry I am about this. I promise that we will deal with Emma, and she will be dealt with properly. Though I hope this doesn't affect our business dealings."

"I have nothing against you and your brothers. But from now on, I just ask that you keep Emma away from me, my wife, and my family. I'll make it a point to let you know when I will be here, and I think it's best that she's not."

"I completely understand, and we'll make sure that she is nowhere around you. Again, I am so sorry." Jasper says and then turns to his sister.

"But I'm not..." Emma starts.

"You will do as you are told as long as you are living in this house. How dare you! Now get your ass inside." Jasper raises his voice, and for the first time, I see fear on Emma's face.

Jasper is a good guy and I know he never raised a hand to her in anger, but I've also never heard him raise his voice either. Emma's made her own bed, and now she's about to reap the consequences of it.

Jasper looks back and nods at me before Willow and I get back into my truck and go home. Once in the car, she still doesn't say a word to me. I keep waiting for her to say something, anything. But as we climb into the mountains, she is still quiet, so when we reach one of the pull offs that are there for those that want to take in the view, I stop. Only then does she finally turn to look at me.

Turning off the truck, I reach and take her hand. Though really I'm wishing I could pull her in to my seat and effectively kill any of the space between us.

"Please talk to me, yell at me, hit me, something," I beg.

Instead, she just sits there staring at me. The longer she goes without saying a word, the more my heart drops. I'm almost certain that I'm about to lose her. I don't know how to stop it or what to do. Though losing her and letting her go is no longer an option.

Maybe she doesn't trust me like I hope she did, or maybe we did rush into this. Though I thought we had built some kind of trust, especially out there on that camping trip and then again on our wedding night.

Finally, she sighs and gives my hand a light squeeze.

"Take me back to the mountain," she says with a softness in her face.

Once again, I start the truck to take us back home.

The entire way there, she doesn't let go of my hand. But the moment I park the truck in the driveway, she forcefully pulls me towards her. I don't even get a chance to speak before her lips are on mine.

This kiss mends everything from the last few hours. This kiss says what we can't seem to say out loud. With this kiss, I try to tell her she is mine forever and I'm not letting her go. This kiss says I'm not letting anyone ever get between us.

We are both breathing hard by the time we break apart. When I get her inside and the door closes behind us, I plan to make love to my wife.

Chapter 14

Emelie

I'm so happy for Bennett that he seems to have found someone. But I can't keep shaking this feeling that Willow is hiding something from us, and possibly even from Bennett.

It took a few days of convincing, but Axel finally took me to visit Phoenix. Besides Jack, Phoenix is the one who is most connected to the outside world. Hopefully, he'll also know how to help me find what I'm looking for, even though I'm not 100% sure exactly what it is I'm searching for.

What I'm hoping to find is something to calm me down and prove she's not here with bad intentions and that she's not going to hurt Bennett.

"It's not too late to back out of this, little one. We can just go home," Axel says as we pull into Phoenix and Jenna's driveway.

"I'm the one that pushed him to start dating online and I can't get rid of this feeling that she's not telling the whole story or leaving something out. If Bennett were to get hurt, it would be all on me."

"Little one, you know it would not be your fault. If Willow is hiding something and Bennett gets hurt in any way, then it's her fault. It will be on Willow and not anything to do with you. You're such a good person and such a good soul that I know you're blaming yourself, but you are blameless. All you were doing is trying to help out our friend. Right now, he is happy and that might have to be enough," Axel says.

While I know it's the code up here that each man stays out of the other one's business, I simply can't let this go. But I don't even have to say it out loud. When I look over at my husband, he knows.

"Fine. Let's at least make this quick so you can go lie down and rest. You've been stressing yourself out way too much about this."

"I can agree with that."

When we get out of the truck, Jenna greets us at the door with a big smile on her face.

"Phoenix told me why you are here, and I want to help. So, I reached out to an old friend and gave him the information that we had on Willow, and he sent me back an email. I haven't read it yet because I wanted to wait until you were here," Jenna says.

Sometimes I forget that Jenna used to have a ton of connections. When she lived in Denver, her parents would network in all the right circles and they were always on all the society pages. But she walked away from that life and from the arranged marriage that her parents tried to set up for her and ended up here in Whiskey River, where she met Phoenix.

So Jenna knows to talk to all the right people. I don't know why I didn't think to ask if she had any connections before, but I'm grateful that she does.

Her laptop is set up at their dining room table, so we gather around. Then she pulls up the email which verifies Willow's name, birthday, and the fact that her father did recently just die, and then there's a link to the only social media profile that the contact was able to find on her.

I feel a lot better knowing that all the basics are true, and that she didn't lie about who she is. Jenna pulls up the link that is in the email and we both gasp at the same time. It's not a social media account like we thought it. Instead, it's kind of set up like a dating profile, only it's a mail-order bride website. The picture displayed is clearly her.

"Why would she marry Bennett if she was trying to set up a mail-order bride scenario?" I ask out loud.

"That's something you're going to have to ask her, little one," Axel says, but his voice is soft as he knows this is not the news that we were hoping to find.

"It should be you that talks to her as you two seemed to really click," Jenna says.

I know she's right because I thought we had a really strong connection.

We say our goodbyes and go home. All this information has given me a lot to think about, and I want to make sure that I approach this the right way. Even though I know my husband is not going to be happy about it, he knows me well and knows I'm not going to stop.

"You're not going to drop this, are you, little one?" He asks once we get home.

"No, I'm not. But I promise to wait a few days and take time to think about how I want to go about this. Deal?"

"That's fair enough," Axel says, pulling me into his arms.

"Now my giant, take me to the river."

· · · · • · • · · ·

As promised, I waited a few days. But now we're going to talk to Willow and Bennett. I've been going over and over in my head what I want to say and her possible reactions or reasons, but everything I come up with leads to things not being good. When I considered letting it go, since Bennett is so happy, I couldn't do it. If he's going to be hurt, I'd rather it be now rather than several years down the road when it's just going to hurt a hell of a lot more.

Since they aren't expecting us, Axel walks up and knocks on the door, knowing that he'll probably have a shotgun in his face when the door opens. It's just how the guys are around here. And I'm right, because there stands Bennett with a shotgun. Though he drops it as soon as he sees us.

"Hey man, everything okay?" Bennett asks as he steps aside for us to come in.

"We're about to find out," Axel says and then nods to me.

With shaky hands, I pull out the folded piece of paper with her mail-order bride profile on it.

"Does Bennett know about this?" I ask, holding the paper open for both of them to see. Though really, I'm watching her more than I watch Bennett. Only it's not the shocked or disgusted look that I was thinking I'd get. Bennett moves to Willow's side and wraps an arm around her waist.

"Yes, I know. It's how we met."

At his words, I look over at Willow, and her eyes are wide and she looks scared.

"Why didn't you just tell us that?" I sigh and sit down on the couch. Axel sits down as close as he possibly can and wraps an arm around me. Though I'm sure if this wasn't a serious conversation, he would have pulled me into his lap instead.

"I wasn't exactly proud of it," Willow says.

"I kept getting this feeling that you were hiding something, and even more so on your wedding day. I wish you had just told us. We wouldn't have cared. You two are obviously happy together and that's what matters. Not how you met."

"I checked out that online dating site that you told me about a while back, but it just wasn't for me. Then I started looking around and came across her profile and reached out. But when I first saw her picture there was this connection I couldn't ignore," Bennett says.

"Kind of like when I first saw you, little one," Axel says, squeezing my hip.

"Why hasn't this profile been taken down? You two are married and you've been for a couple weeks now," I ask.

"We emailed them a copy of the marriage certificate, basically proving that we fulfilled the contract. It's on them to take it down it. I'm sure it will be gone soon. Unfortunately, I don't have any control over the profile itself," Willow says.

"Well, we need to have lunch with the girls so that you can fill them in, too. We're all going to want to know why you did it and about your life before you moved out here," I tell her.

"I didn't lie about anything," Willow says with a glint of defiance in her eyes. "I came out here because my dad died, and I had no one and nothing. That part is all true. I just went about it a little differently." She shrugs like it's no big deal.

"But really, it kind of is. It's not the traditional route someone uses to find someone," I say.

Out of the corner of my eye, I notice that Bennett and Axel are exchanging a few silent looks. So there might be more to the story they're not sharing.

"Then I have one question for you. Have you been up front and told Bennett everything? I don't care if you tell me or tell the rest of the girls, but I want to make sure that he knows everything." I say to her and watch closely for a reaction.

For the fraction of a second, I swear I see guilt in her eyes but replaced quickly with a smile as she turns to Bennett.

"He knows all the important things, but we're still learning about each other too," she says, smiling up at him.

It's a copout answer, but I guess I'll let it go for now.

We make plans for lunch and then leave.

Once back in the truck heading home, I'm thinking over everything she said.

"What was Bennett trying to tell you?" I ask. Axel has no emotion on his face when he says, "It was a look that said he didn't want to talk about it right now."

"So, she is still hiding something. I hope for his sake that she has at least told Bennett what it is."

And I hope for her sake that she'll open up about it so that we can help her.

Chapter 15

Willow

Emelie wouldn't let me push the lunch out with the girls too long. She insisted it be within a week. So, I'm in town today having lunch at the cafe with them. This is the first time I've ventured out on my own. Bennett wasn't a fan of me coming into town by myself, but I assured him that I felt safe and that this was something that I needed to do. He agreed and reminded me to go to Jack if I needed anything. Even so, he still wasn't happy about me coming into town without him and offered multiple times to drive me in and then hang out with Jack while we have lunch. But I told him no because I refuse to let my past control me.

Driving the mountain by myself is a little nerve-wracking. It's pretty steep and curvy in several places, so like I promised Bennett, I took it slow, and I didn't rush. Though I've never been quite so happy to park the truck and get out.

When I walk into the cafe, I'm still a few minutes early, but all the girls are already there at the table waiting for me. At this point, I'm assuming they've all already seen the profile, as I'm sure Emelie has shared the details. Really, I don't mind. I'm actually relieved to have it in the open, even if it sucks that I'm not telling them everything.

When Emelie was making sure that at least Bennett knew the truth, I felt guilty. But I don't feel like I lied to her. He does know the important parts, and he's made it clear he knows I'm running from something or hiding from something.

I've thought about it a lot over the last few days, and I've decided that it's time to tell Bennett the truth. In my mind, I've been going over what I want to say, making sure that I have all the details sorted out because I've been trying to forget about it up until now. But that's something to worry about later. Right now, I need to get through lunch.

As soon as Emelie sees me, she gets up, walks over to me, and gives me a huge hug. She has a big smile on her face, so I'm hoping that's a good sign for today.

"We waited to order until you got here. But let's get food first and then we'll chat because we're all starving," she says, leading me back to the table.

As we order food, everyone is super friendly and we're catching up. But once the order is placed, everyone turns to look at me.

"Listen, I want to start with I never truly lied to you guys, I just didn't tell you about the mail-order bride thing. Bennett and I met online. My dad died leaving me with nothing and I was living in a woman's shelter for a while. One of the girls there told me about this website. Since I didn't want to stay in Chicago, it sounded like a good idea. I never expected Bennett, though." I can't stop the smile that crosses my face if I tried.

"So why not just tell us that from the beginning?" Hope asks.

"Can you honestly tell me that you had a good reaction when you first heard that we met on a mail-order bride website? Or can you tell me you didn't judge me right away even if you stopped yourself? There's a stigma attached to having met there and I get it, but I wanted to get to know you all first because I knew how important you are to Bennett."

No one really says anything, but the girls look around at each other and thankfully, this is also when they deliver our food.

"So, you lived in Chicago with your dad?" Jenna asks.

"Yeah, my mom bailed a long time ago. It was just me and my dad for as long as I can remember. I was very much daddy's little girl and then he got sick with cancer, so I took care of him. He had some money saved up, but between it and the house, it was just enough to pay off his medical bills."

"How long were you in the woman's shelter?" Emelie asks.

"A few weeks. When I was taking my dad to chemo, I met a girl who was taking her mom. We became friends and when her mom passed away, she let me stay with her. Eventually, she became my best friend because she really was the only one who understood what I was going through."

"Why didn't you stay there with her?" Jana asks.

"She was in much the same position, except she was determined not to sell her house. So, she ended up doing something a bit crazy as well." I cringe because I know what the next question is going to be.

"What did she do?" they all ask at the same time.

"She ahh... entered an auction at a club up there. This sandwich is really good." I say after taking a bite.

"What kind of auction? And what kind of club?" Hope asks.

"It's a BDSM club, and it was a virgin auction," I tell them quickly, ripping off the Band-Aid.

"A virgin... auction... like where she auctioned off her virginity?" Jenna asks.

"Yeah." I cringe again because I can only imagine what's going through their heads.

"How did that go for her?" Hope asks.

"Honestly, I'm not sure. I was going to stop by Jack's place before I head home and shoot her an email with Bennett's phone number. When she gets a chance, we can talk and catch up and I'll get all the details. The auction would have taken place recently, so I have no idea if she even went through with it. The last I heard she was meeting with them to sign the contract and that was the day I left town."

"I had no idea things like that even existed," Emelie says clearly in shock.

"Well, I didn't even know mail-order brides were still a thing until they told me about the website, so that makes two of us. I'm honestly going to be shocked if she was able to go through with it. But her house means a lot to her, so I kind of think she did." I tell them honestly.

I really like these girls and I promise to be as honest with them as I can after this. Because I know having people you can count on up on the mountain is going to be a big thing, and I have every intention of staying.

The conversation flows and we talk about anything and everything. Each of the girls shares their story about how they came to be on the mountain. Turns out, I'm not the only one that was running away from something either.

After our meal, we all walk out to the parking lot together and there are a lot of hugs exchanged.

"We aren't happy that you lied, and we hate that you felt like you had to, but we understand. Just know that we are here for you and all we ask is the truth. But we won't ever pull anything out of you that you're not wanting to talk about either." Emelie says in a way that makes me wonder if she has a feeling there's more to the story.

It surprises me that Bennett and Emelie are the two people who seem to be able to read me like a damn book, whether I want them to or not.

After we say our goodbyes, I hop in the truck and drive down the road to Jack's shop. When I step in, Jack greets me with a warm smile, but he looks behind me as if he's looking for Bennett.

"Just you? Is everything okay?" he asks.

"Yeah, I was in town having lunch with the girls and wanted to stop by and see if I could use a computer to send an email really quick?"

"Oh, of course. Come here and let me show you." He takes me to the backroom where the desktop is set up and shows me how to log in.

"You can use this one anytime you want. Bennett uses it as well. If you're looking to order anything, let me know and I'll do that for you.

Many times I can get a discount with my retail accounts."

"Thanks, but I'm just sending an email to check in on a friend, but I'll keep that in mind. I might be needing some more fabric soon," I tell him with a smile, and he leaves me to it.

I sign into my email hoping maybe there's already something from Aspen, but after sorting through and deleting all the junk there isn't one.

Quickly, I send her an email with the phone number Bennett gave me to the house and tell her to call me as soon as she's able. Then I assure her that everything is fine, but I still want to know how she's doing.

With the email sent, all I can do is wait. After thanking Jack, I send up a silent prayer that she'll call soon.

Chapter 16

Bennett

When Willow walks in the door, I'm just finishing making some bread. She's all smiles, so I assume it went well. Happy to see her home safely, I walk over and greet her with a hug and a kiss.

"Hey, sweetheart, how did lunch go?"

"It went better than I had hoped it would. We talked and I explained and they made me promise to tell the truth from now on. Of course I did as I really like them. I explained why I did the mail-order bride thing and how I found out about it. Then we talked about my dad. All in all I feel like it was a good conversation," she says with her arms still wrapped around me.

"Good. I'm glad you girls worked it out. They'll go home and tell their husbands and I'm sure I'll hear about it if they have any questions in a day or two. But up here in the mountains, we tend to not ask too many questions. Well, I think, at least the guys don't. They'll just take it for what it is."

"Whatever you're making smells delicious," she says, letting go of me and heading into the kitchen.

"We're running low on bread, so I made some. It kept me busy, so I didn't think too much about how you were down in town all by yourself. Oh, by the way, you got a phone call while you were gone."

Her eyes light up and I guess maybe she had been waiting for the phone call.

"Aspen called that fast? I only just sent the email before I left town. Did she leave a number where I can call her back?" she asks.

"It was not Aspen, it was your uncle," I tell her as I go to the phone to grab the piece of paper I wrote his contact information on.

When I look back at Willow, she's completely spooked. She's white and seems to be having a panic attack. I can't get to her side fast enough. But when I do, she collapses into my arms and I'm able to get her to the couch.

"How the hell did he find me?" she gasps.

"Calm down. Take a deep breath. You two aren't close? He made it seem like you were. I thought you gave him the number." I say while trying to figure out exactly what's going on here.

"No, I want nothing to do with him," she says, taking a few more deep breaths.

"All right. That's it. I'll deal with it. You don't have anything to worry about. If he calls again, I'll keep him away from you."

As I hold Willow in my arms, her breathing steadies and she begins to calm down. I have so many questions running through my head. Why would he pretend that they were close? If just the mention of her uncle elicits this kind of a response from her, and upsets her this much, why hasn't she told me about it?

It takes a while, but she finally regains her composure.

"Why don't you go do some quilting? I'll take care of dinner tonight." I tell her, suggesting something that I know she loves to do.

But she doesn't say anything. Nodding, she goes over to the sewing table and it's like she's completely shut down.

For the rest of the day, she's off, not herself. She doesn't talk much and I catch her staring off into nothing. Every time I ask if she's okay, she nods, but there's no real emotion on her face.

It's like she's here, but she's not. At the dinner table, she sits with me, but mostly pushes her food around. When she catches me watching her, she takes a few bites, but I'm assuming she's only eating to appease me. I'd give anything to know what's going through her head right now, but every time I ask a question, she just shrugs or shakes her head. Since she got home and found out that her uncle had called, she hasn't spoken. I'm starting to worry and I'm not sure what to do.

We go to bed early and I figure I'll wait and see how she is in the morning before I make any decisions. If this continues, I can always call Cole since he has medic training. He might have some suggestions or ideas.

Lying there side by side, neither of us speaks, but she at least lets me hold her hand. With that small connection, I feel slightly better.

I can tell the moment she falls asleep, because her body finally relaxes. Hopefully, things will look different in the morning. Because I know I won't be able to handle another day like this.

As I'm drifting off to sleep, Willow begins moving around. I'm wondering if she's getting up to go to the bathroom when I hear a blood-curdling scream coming from her.

• • • • • • • • • •

Willow

I'm watching myself at my dad's funeral. It's like one of those out-of- body experiences. I'm in my black dress and all our friends are there offering condolences and trying to be nice. They're telling me if they could help in any way to let them know. Then I see my aunt and uncle, who are attempting to run the show as if they were any part of my dad's life. Acting like they are a grieving family member when, in fact, my dad's own sister wasn't there for him when he lay dying. In fact, they haven't talked in years.

As I watch all the guests slowly leave, my aunt goes into the kitchen to clean up. She's attempting to look like she's actually helping and impress the few that are left who are talking to my uncle. Without thinking, I go upstairs to my dad's room and stand in the doorway looking at how everything is in the exact same place that he left it. His sweatshirt is hanging on the back of the chair in the corner that he liked to sit in and read. He always took it with him when he went to get chemo because he'd say how cold they kept the place.

In my mind's eye, I can see every detail. His cologne is on the dresser, his watch on the nightstand, and even the last book he was reading sitting on the side of the bed where my mom used to sleep.

Wanting to get a smell of him, maybe even his cologne, I step into the room. I'm yelling at myself not to do it. Don't step into that room alone. Turn around, hurry, and go back downstairs.

With every step I take into my dad's room, I try to yell louder at myself.

"Willow! Wake up! Willow!" A far off voice is calling my name. Though it gets closer and closer and then louder.

The moment I opened my eyes, I realize I was having a dream, well, more like a nightmare. I was back in that horrible day, and right now my husband's alarmed look is what greets me.

"Sweetheart, you've got to tell me what's going on. It's affecting you so much that you're screaming out in your sleep. Please tell me. Open up to me and let me help you."

Bennett is pleading with me, raw emotion filling his face and voice. Turning myself into his chest, I start ugly crying. Holding me tightly, he rubs my back and kisses the top of my head. I finally let our all this emotion, soaking his chest with my tears. I've had to be strong for so long and I'm tired, so tired. Eventually, my sobbing turns from emotion to release. Then guilt hits me for keeping this from him for so long.

"I'm so sorry... I was going to tell you... I'm so sorry... I'm so... so sorry..." I blubber into his chest as I try to get my words out.

"You didn't have to tell me anything you didn't want to, I told you that and I meant it. Even though I still mean it, if it's affecting you this much, I think it's going to be better for you to get it out. Why don't you lean on me for a change?"

"Growing up," I begin. "It was just my dad and me. The only family he had left was his sister, who was married to some high-up politician. They never got along and for the longest time, they never even talked. At the time of my dad's funeral, they hadn't seen each other in over five years. Nothing. They didn't talk, and he was happy to have her out of our lives. Once when I asked my dad why, he said she changed when she married the politician. Also, he told me they just weren't good people. I trusted my dad, and I never had any reason to question it."

The memories from the nightmare are still so vivid in my head. This is the last thing I want to be talking about. Yet I know it needs to happen.

"The day of the funeral, my aunt and uncle showed up as if they had been this loving family to my dad his whole life. They acted like they were the ones that helped him through his cancer and that they were there when he died. Most of our friends knew it wasn't true. Everyone there knew my father didn't have a relationship with his sister and so we all just ignored her. Because heaven forbid the politician and his wife didn't show up to her brother's funeral. It was a publicity stunt, but I just didn't have the energy to call her out on it or deal with it, so I let them stay.

As everyone was leaving, my aunt started cleaning the kitchen and putting on a show for the last few people that were there. I disappeared up to my dad's room. I had left it just the way he had. Everything was in the same place that he had left it. But I was missing him so much and all I wanted was to smell his cologne and pretend for a moment he was alive. Maybe he would walk into his room and hug me. Unfortunately, it was not him that walked into the room. It was my uncle.

After he closed the door behind him, he used his body to block my exit. Then he started saying all this stuff about how he knew about my dad's medical bills and how my dad had asked him to take care of me. Without a doubt, I knew it was all absolute bullshit because my father had been preparing me to take care of myself and he would have never asked my uncle to take care of me. Of all the people that he could have reached out to, he would rather have asked the stranger off the street than my uncle and I knew it.

As my uncle talked, he would get closer and closer to me. Even though I tried to move away, he wouldn't let me. He kept spouting on about how I was now his responsibility and kept talking as if I was his property.

When he got close enough, he grabbed my arm and threw me face-first down on the bed."

I squeeze my eyes shut not wanting to remember what happened next and I can feel Bennett's entire body tense.

"He got his pants open and my dress flipped up. I was struggling to escape and not making any headway. He hit me a few times and then when my aunt came in to talk to him, I used that moment to get away. Of course, I called the police because there were refusing to leave the house. Even after I filed the report, and they took photos of my injuries, the bruises and a busted lip, he should have been charged at least for assault. But it got buried because he's a high-powered politician and has some bad cops in his back pocket.

Though they did make him leave the house and told him to stay away from me because it would be better for his campaign if he wasn't connected to me. But that's all they did.

The judge wouldn't even give me a restraining order. I pitched a fit to any police officer that would listen, and I guess I pitched enough of a fit that I caught my uncle's attention. Then he started calling me, making threats about how I better change my story and how nothing happened, and it wasn't what I was making it out to be.

After that, I packed up anything I wanted to keep, selling the rest, and sold the house to pay off my dad's medical bills. Then I went into a women's shelter that had security. When I told them what happened, they made sure that my uncle wasn't allowed anywhere near the building. Then Aspen invited me to stay with her, which was great because my uncle didn't know about her. That was my main reason to sign up for the mail-order bride website. I wanted out of Chicago at any cost. Even if it meant marrying some old fat ugly man and having a mundane life being nothing more than his housemaid."

"Well, you're here now and I will protect you, no matter what. Even from fancy politicians. We do things a lot differently here on the mountain and you're not alone anymore. Not only do you have me, but you have eight other people that will make sure that you are safe and many more in town who will protect you without even knowing you."

"I'm sorry I didn't tell you sooner. I was really scared that you wouldn't want this kind of trouble at your doorstep, and you'd kick me out and move on. The longer I went without telling you, the harder it became. For what it's worth, I had made the decision to tell you before I had lunch with the girls. But that phone call threw everything off."

Chapter 17

Bennett

The next morning, the first thing I did was call the guys on the radio and let them know what was going on. Within an hour, they were gathered in my living room with their wives. I love that we have such a support team around us. Willow gives them a much shorter version of the story of what happened with her uncle and how he called while she was out yesterday.

The girls jump up and instantly surround her, offering her support, comfort, and protection. Watching these girls circle around my wife and give her this kind of friendship, something which I know she's never had before, makes me a bit choked up.

Once they all sit down again, Hope tells her story of how her mom had kidnapped both her and Jana and how we men went in and saved them. After the guys each give their girls a kiss, they join me on the other side of the room.

"So, what's the plan?" Axel asks as he crosses his arms and stares at me.

"Honestly, I don't know. As far as we know, her uncle is still in Chicago, but now he knows she's lives here. There's no telling if he'll actually come out here or not. Maybe with any luck, he'll think that Montana is far enough away and he'll let it be," I say hopefully.

"My experience with guys like that is that they won't give up. They want to make sure that there's nothing or no one that can ruin their reputation," Phoenix says, and his wife Jenna agrees. Since they both came from a high society background before they settled on the mountain, they have the most experience with people like Willow's uncle.

"I brought a bunch of my brother's cameras and tracking equipment. I think we should set them up around your house. Though we'll have to make sure that we're continuously monitoring them so we can catch the first signs of anything out of place," Cash says.

His brother was extremely paranoid about the government coming after him for some of his ideas. In fact, he was so paranoid that when he was diagnosed with cancer, he refused treatment and then died several months later. Shortly after, Cash met Hope and used all of his brother's equipment to help protect her.

"If you see any signs of someone being here, you call me," Cole says.

He's a man of few words, but we do know he's prior military and one hell of a tracker. When Hope and Jana were taken, he's the one that tracked them down and helped us save them. Also, that's how he met Jana and the two have been inseparable since.

"All right, let's get anything that we can set up. The better I can protect her, the better I'll feel. Though I hesitate about leaving the girls alone inside the house, even if we're just outside."

Thankfully, Axel seems to understand.

"I'll stay inside with them," he says.

The rest of us nod before we head out. It's great to be with men who understand how protective we are of our women. Men that I can trust, and I know will protect her if the time comes.

Going around outside, we set up several cameras to watch the house. Then we place several more from the woods, watching entry points like the driveway and even the back of the house, in case he tries to come in from the other side of my property.

"I think we should set up a few down by the road. This road isn't well traveled, so anyone out here would have a reason to be on it, and you know your neighbors, right?" Cole asks.

"Yeah, there's just one guy at the end of the road, and there's a few abandoned cabins. But no one ever visits them anymore, so anything outside of my neighbor would be enough of a red flag to check out," I say.

Then we get to work. Cash and Phoenix go down to the road and set up some hunting cameras there while we work near the house. Cash sets up a driveway alarm, so we'll have at least a little notice when anyone comes up the driveway in a vehicle, anyway.

We install some extra locks on the doors of not just the house but the outbuildings as well. That way, if she happens to be outside and needs to get somewhere safe, it doesn't have to be the house.

Everything that we have to do and consider makes my mind spin. But if it means keeping her safe, then it's not even a question whether we do it or not. After several hours, we get everything set up. When we finally come back inside, I can see the relief in Willow's eyes. It looks like she doesn't like being away from me any more than I like being away from her.

"Just stay alert and vigilant, and we'll see you guys in a couple of days when we meet at Jack's shop," Axel says and they head out.

Now, Willow refuses to leave my side. If I'm going outside, so does she. I'm completely okay with that because at least if she's with me and I have eyes on her, I know she's all right. Though I'm glad she went in and had lunch with the girls when she did, because there's no way I'd be able to allow her to go into town now by herself. I don't think she'd want to either.

· · · · ● · ● · · ·

Willow

Ever since I told him the story about my uncle, Bennett has been comforting me. I'm relieved that he's been fine with me attached to his side. The thought of him being out of my sight scares me and I can't stand it. Even though the guys went through so much trouble to make the house extra safe, that bubble of safety I had just last week is gone. But I so desperately want it back.

Today we're heading into town to see the guys at Jack's shop. Also, we'll be dropping off some of our stuff for sale, including my first quilt to see how they do in the shop. Bennett has made it very clear that it doesn't matter if the quilts sell. Even if they don't, I can keep making them to give away as presents or donate them to people in need. He says if quilting makes me happy, then I should keep doing it. One way or another, it doesn't matter what happens with the quilts. That right there means everything to me. Even in the midst of all this, he's so set on my happiness.

We are one of the first ones to the shop, so Jack checks over my quilt. Then we talk about the cost of materials versus what we would need to make in order for all of us to make a profit. Finally, we land on a price that we decide to try. After inputting into his system and pricing it, he puts it on the floor.

By that time, the other couples are coming in and dropping their stuff off. The guys ask how things have been up at the house and if we've had any problems. But it's been quiet, not that my nerves have understood because they're still in full force.

Since Jack is a lawyer, we tell him about what's going on and if he has any advice.

"These are the exact type of people that I did not want to work for and that I wanted to protect people against. They are the ones who abuse and manipulate the system to get what they want. If you're okay with it, I'd like to do some research and see what I can come up with," Jack says.

I agree and give him everything I know about my uncle, from his address to the phone number that he left for Bennett. I include my aunt's name and the police station where I filed the report.

Before we even leave the store, my quilt sells. We all stand there in shock as the customer gushes over it and how hard it is to find handmade quilts nowadays, but she loves the local fabrics that were used in the construction of it. When she leaves, the girls all turn to me and Jack laughs.

"It looks like we underpriced ourselves. I'm willing to bet we could price it at another hundred dollars and they'd still sell. So, I'll take as many as you can make."

"Would you be willing to teach us how to quilt?" Hope asks.

"I'd love to! Let's get together in the afternoons and quilt and talk. Though it would have to be after this hunting trip the guys have been talking about," I say and they all agree.

"You ready to go, sweetheart? Cash and Cole are going to follow us home and make sure everything is still okay."

And just like that, my nerves that had started to go away talking to the girls flare and are back in full force.

We get into the truck to go home and are followed by Cash and Cole in their trucks. But the closer we get to the house, the stronger the sinking feeling in the pit of my stomach gets.

"I have a bad feeling." I whisper because I'm a worried that giving it words is going to make it come true. Then Bennett grips my hand a little tighter and glances at me for just a moment before his eyes are back on the road.

"So do I," he says and we're both quiet the rest of the drive.

Once we pull into the driveway, nothing looks out of place. After Bennett checks the house, everything is still secure and the way we left it.

Bennett turns to me. "Stay here while we go check outside."

"I'm not leaving your side." If I have to, I'm not above begging. Thankfully, he takes one look at me, nods and I follow him outside to meet up with the men. Their wives are waiting in the car both with a gun on their lap and I'm pretty sure the car doors are locked as well.

We walk around the house and then to the tree line around the driveway before we meet back up with Cash and Cole, who were checking some cameras.

"Someone's definitely been here," Cole says. "From the looks of it, they didn't even step out of the tree line. I almost wonder if they saw one of the cameras and then left. There's no face shot or really any good shot at all."

My body goes cold because in my gut I have an idea of who it is. Though I don't want to believe that he's actually here in Montana and that he would go this far. I'm praying against all reason that it's just some hiker that got lost.

Almost like Bennett knows where my mind is going, he wraps an arm around my waist.

"Let's get you inside." Without waiting for me to move, he simply swoops down, picks me up, and carries me inside.

Chapter 18

Bennett

As soon as Axel and Phoenix heard that someone had been here, they dropped everything and came over. Right now we're sitting here formulating a plan. We set up some more security cameras that Phoenix brought over.

"I think we should cancel this hunting trip. I'm not willing to leave the girls alone." I tell the guys, and they start nodding in agreement. But apparently, the girls have other plans.

"Absolutely fucking not," Willow says, and my head snaps to her. I've never heard her cuss other than a few damns and what the hells. So, to hear that strong word coming from her grabs my attention.

The other women quickly agree with her and try to stare us down.

"We don't need to cancel the trip. Just take us with you," Emelie says like it's the most obvious answer in the world.

Looking around at the other guys, who are nodding their heads at each other, it doesn't take a genius to see that we all agree. It's the best of both worlds. We still get our hunting trip, and we can take the girls with us.

"We'll have to make a few adjustments to our plans, but I think it's for the best." Phoenix says, and we all agree.

The only reason we were going hunting without them is because the girls had plans to have some girl time together, but I think we're all in agreement that we'd rather have our girls with us anyway.

We spend the next hour adjusting our plans for the trip to include the women. One of the major changes was bringing the tents instead of camping out under the sky like we had been planning. While we're discussing the changes, the girls are making plans on what they're going to do.

Finally, they decide they'll hunt with us one morning and then take some of the girl time they had planned down by the lake.

After we had finalized our plans, we said goodbye to our friends.

I turn to Willow, "Come on let's go out back because I want to make sure that you can shoot, though not just for the hunting trip."

She follows me out the back door and away from the house where there's a fallen tree and I set up a few things for her to use for target practice.

Then I begin showing her how to shoot the guns I have including my hunting rifle, the shotgun I keep by the door, and the handgun that is on the nightstand by our bed. She is a little nervous at first, which is the exact reason that we need to be practicing. Though the more comfortable and confident she gets with her shooting, the better her aim gets.

By the time we're done practicing, she's pretty confident no matter which of the guns she picks up. Also, I feel more satisfied that she can protect herself if the need arises. Even though I have every intention of being right there to do it for her.

"We'll practice more each day before the hunting trip," I say. But the trip is in three days, and I really hope that's enough.

* * *

Willow

Today we're on the hunting trip and if I felt safe with Bennett around, I feel extra safe with five guys with guns surrounding me. A major bonus is the kick-ass girls who are here too for moral support.

This trip is exactly what Ben and I needed. It's a chance to focus on something else while knowing our best friends have our backs.

"Okay, we're going to get you girls set up at the lake and we're going to go scout the area." Phoenix says as the lake comes into view.

The guys have the tents set up quickly, honestly faster than I thought possible for one person to set up one tent. Meanwhile, the girls and I are getting lunch together. Before we left, we had packed some sandwiches for today and supplies for breakfast while we're here. But lunch and dinner are going to be completely dependent on what we're able to catch.

After some discussion, the girls and I plan to try our hand at some fishing. Cash has set up some traps for smaller animals, but the big hunt is tomorrow. After we eat and the guys head out, the girls and I lay blankets down on the beach by the lake to get a little sun and talk. It's been unseasonably warm, and we plan to take advantage of it.

"This is the one thing I miss about Georgia. You can pretty much lay out any time of the year, get tan and soak up the sun," Hope says.

"Not here, sweetheart. Seventy-five percent of the year you'd freeze your ass off," Jana says, and we all laugh.

"Same thing in Chicago. If a woman had a tan, it probably came from a tanning bed," I tell them, which elicits some more laughs.

"I'd use a self-tanner if I wasn't scared of coming out looking like a carrot," Emelie adds.

We all laughingly agree and then the topic moves on to books and setting up the quilting date.

The weekend seems to fly by. I enjoyed being out hunting with Bennett, but I also loved the time with the girls just as much.

Before I know it, we're eating breakfast and planning to make the hike back to the cabin.

"We should make this a yearly camping trip," I suggest. We've had so much fun. I'm not quite ready for everything to end. Since each of the guys got an elk, we have no other option but to go home.

Everyone likes the idea of an annual camping trip. After that, we break up camp and start the trek back home. Surprisingly, the hike doesn't seem to take as long to get back to the cabin as it did to get out to the lake.

But once there, I stop dead in my tracks.

Our cabin has been broken into and the doors are wide open. I know we locked them because both of us double checked before we left.

The guys and Bennett drop everything and go inside while Cole stays with us. If I had to stand by anybody but Bennett for protection, it would be Cole. He's serious and with the scar on his face he can appear deadly.

The house has definitely been rifled through, but it doesn't look like anything is missing. Tire tracks at the front lead up to the house and then straight back out.

"Axel is calling Detective Greer down at the police station because he's worked with us before." Bennett says as he comes back to join us.

"Make sure you tell him about all the issues you had with your uncle. For one thing, he's on our side and the more he knows, the easier it'll be to protect you. Possibly he'll be able to put a stop to your uncle messing with you legally anyway," Cole says, looking down at the gun in his hands.

It seems like forever before the cops show up, and thankfully, Bennett takes the lead. He fills them in on what happened and what's been going on with my uncle, the phone call and threats. Then I step in and tell them what happened with my uncle at my dad's funeral, the police reports I tried to file, and the districts that dismissed them.

Detective Greer takes a ton of notes. He asks me who I talked to at the police stations, which precincts I filed with, and when. Finally, he asks some questions that I'm not quite sure how they're relevant, like when we got married and when we met. That sort of thing.

"The fact that he's friends with the sheriff out there means nothing here. So I'm going to do some poking around and see if I can get copies of those filed reports, which will be to our benefit if it is indeed him who's behind this," Greer says.

"I'm glad that you're the last one to get married because you guys seem to attract trouble in droves. Hopefully, after this, it will calm down." Though he's kind of serious, I can tell with the smirk on his face that he's also playing around with us too.

Now if only the pit in my stomach would go away, along with the feeling that this is far from over, I would feel better.

Chapter 19

Bennett

It's been a few days since the break in and the guys and the girls are back at our house again. Willow insists on trying to keep things as normal as possible, which meant keeping the quilting date that the girls had planned. Right now, she's teaching them some quilting tricks and tips in the living room, while the guys and I are in my office.

It's been pretty quiet over the last few days, but Willow and I both said we have a feeling this isn't over. From what I know about her uncle and the bit of research that Phoenix did, I have to agree.

"Jana was asking in town if they've heard anything or if anything has been leaked about Willow's uncle. So far, it's been quiet. Thankfully, the cops are keeping this on the down low," Cole says.

Since Jana used to live in town and managed a grocery store in the café, she's a great resource. She also runs the community garden, which has now been moved to their property. If anyone has solid connections in town, it's her.

"Right now, I'm relieved that things are quiet," I say.

"Just because it's been quiet, don't let your guard down. That was my mistake." Cash says, and I know he's talking about when his wife's mom kidnapped her. There had been signs, and they knew her mom was in town, but once things got quiet, they relaxed and that's when her mom swooped in.

In that rescue mission to save Hope, we all banded together. Also, it's what brought Cole into our group as well.

"I remember. But I have no intention of letting my guard down anytime soon. From what I know about her uncle, he's going to play the long game. I would bet that he's going to wait for us to relax our vigilance." I say, and the men agree.

Wrapping up our meeting, we go to the living room. Then sitting down, we talk and watch the girls.

When giggles erupt from the girls across the room, I turn to watch Willow. She's got a huge smile lighting up her face, which causes me to grin too. I absolutely love it when she's happy. Even with everything going on, seeing her smile makes everything completely worth it.

I turn back to the guys, and they're all wearing matching grins on their faces and watching their girls across the room. There's no doubt these are my people. We are absolutely content to sit here and be in the same space as our women as they do what they love.

When the phone rings, the entire room freezes, and everyone looks at me. Sending up a silent prayer, I hope that it's Willow's friend that she's been waiting for a phone call from and not bad news.

"Hello," I answer. Unfortunately, it's not a female voice that greets me, it's Jasper's.

"Hey man, I hate to make this phone call, but Emma just came in from town saying that there was some female down there asking around about Willow."

As he talks, I wave Willow over to me, and she comes to my side without hesitating.

"Can you describe this woman who was asking about Willow?" I ask. Willow's eyes go wide and I can see the panic written all over her face. So I wrap my arm around her and pull her to my side, letting her know I'm not going anywhere.

"When she told Emma that she was her aunt, Emma told her where to find you. Knowing how you don't like people just showing up on your doorstep, I thought I should give you a heads up," Jasper says.

Willow trembles in my arms, and I've never wanted to physically injure a woman more than I do Emma right now. Who gives an address to a complete stranger?

"Thanks, Jasper, I appreciate it."

I end the call with him, and turn to the guys, who I'm grateful are now still here.

"Apparently, Emma told some strange woman in town claiming to be Willow's aunt where to find her up here on the mountain," I tell them.

"Emma, the sister of the ranchers you work with?" Axel asks.

"Yep, that was her brother calling to let me know."

"This would be the aunt that is married to the uncle that we're having issues with?" Phoenix asks.

It doesn't escape me that he assumes that our problem is his problem, just like that. No questions asked.

"Yes, the only aunt I have is my dad's sister," Willow says shakily.

"Well, at least we now know she's in town. Let's assume your uncle would be with her," Cole says, and we all agree.

"It's the perfect cover. Women aren't seen as threatening as men, so it makes sense to have her going around asking about you," I say, mostly thinking out loud.

No sooner do I finish my sentence, than there's a knock on the door. From the outside looking in, you'd swear we had this planned and choreographed.

Axel takes Willow's hand and walks her back over to the other women. Then the men put themselves between the door and the girls. I grab my gun as I get ready to answer the door.

Looking around, everybody nods, and I open the door. Expecting to find her aunt on the other side, instead it's a man. Instantly, I know this is her uncle, without ever having met him or seen a photo of him before.

"I'm her uncle and I am here to see Willow. We've been worried about her since her father's funeral. The way she up and disappeared, she's obviously not stable." The man in front of me says this without even offering me his name or asking mine.

So, he's going to play the 'she's unstable game' to make it seem like any of her decisions or anything she says isn't worth a damn. Somehow, that doesn't surprise me. I can tell the moment the men step up behind me because her uncle's eyes go wide for a fraction of a moment before he regains his composure. Without a doubt, I know they want to get a good look at him and know who we are dealing with.

"More like you're worried about her opening her mouth and telling everyone what you did to her," I say. In that moment, he realizes I know what happened and his entire demeanor changes.

"That girl is mentally unstable and has no idea what she's talking about. She needs to be at home with her family," he says in a tone that I'm sure is meant to scare some people.

"Not only is she perfectly stable, but she's my wife, and I am her family. She will be staying here, and you will be leaving her alone. This is your one and only warning. If you step foot on my property again, I will put a bullet between your eyes. See these men here with me? They live all over this mountain and if you accidentally step foot on one of their properties, they'll do the same thing," I tell him without losing eye contact.

Then Axel steps forward and stands right next to me. I'm a tall man at over six feet tall, but Axel is pushing seven feet. If you don't know him, he can look to be one scary son of a bitch, even though he's one of the nicest guys you'll ever meet. But he also knows when to use his size to his advantage, like right now.

The moment Axel steps up to my side, her uncle takes a step backward. Fighting back a smile, all I can think is how cowardly this man truly is.

Then I raise my gun, point it directly at him, cock the trigger, and growl, "Now get off my property."

Chapter 20

Bennett

Answering a knock on the door with my shotgun in hand I find Detective Geer standing there. He was a huge help when Hope and Jana were kidnapped and have taken the men up here on the mountain under his wing and we all appreciate it.

"Bennett," he says.

I lower my shotgun and invite him in.

"Listen, Willow's uncle came into the station saying that you kidnapped her and that you're holding her against her will," he says.

I know the instant Willow pops up beside me because she starts talking.

"No, I ran away from my uncle and came here where Bennett and I were married. It was both of our choices, and he's not holding me against my will. You know this." She sounds panicked and I hate that.

Wrapping my arm around her waist, I hope it will help calm her down. I trust Greer and I know that everything will be all right, even if it doesn't seem like it right now.

"I know all that, but I need you both to come down to the station and give a statement. That way, we will have it on file. Though it's not going to be fun, and you will have to be questioned in separate rooms. We have to do this by the book so that it can't be used against you later. I know the type of person your uncle is and I think we have a long fight ahead of us. Everyone at the station is willing to make that fight with you, but we have to do it the correct way."

Greer says this with such sincerity in his voice that we can't help but trust him. All of this is difficult because I want to be the one to protect her. Now I have to hand it off to someone else.

"Okay, let me call the guys. Then we will follow you in," I tell him, and Willow's eyes go wide.

"It's all right, Willow. We had to go through this with Axel and Emelie. They will ask us some questions on the record, and we will be home for dinner tonight." I hope I'm telling her the truth, so I look over at Detective Greer who nods to me.

A quick call to Phoenix and he lets me know he'll call the other guys and Jack to meet us down at the station.

Then we begin the drive into town. The whole way there, I can feel Willow's nerves. I try to comfort her best that I can by holding her hand and letting her know I'm there for her.

Once we arrive at the police station, we're put in separate rooms, just like we expected to be. With my nervous energy, it's impossible to sit at the table, so I pace around the room. I hate being away from Willow, knowing she's nervous and scared and that there's nothing I can do about it.

It seems like an eternity before Greer steps into the room. He goes through the whole spiel of who he is and why we're here before sitting down at the table. Only then do I sit down even though I still have way too much nervous energy to be sitting still.

"How did you and Willow meet?"

"On an online dating website."

"Were you aware that her uncle was a politician?"

"Not until she told me after we were married."

He nods and takes some notes.

"How long did you and Willow date before you got married?"

"We talked long distance for a few weeks and then she came out here. After a few weeks, we decided to get married."

"How many weeks? One, two, three?"

"I don't know how many weeks we talked, but she came out here about two weeks before we got married."

"And that was a rushed wedding?"

Even though I know he has to ask certain questions based on the claims that her uncle is making, I get irritated. Especially because it's easy to make what we have seem wrong.

"It wasn't rushed. Neither of us wanted a huge wedding. She didn't have any family to invite, and I didn't either, so we celebrated with our friends."

"So, her aunt and uncle were not invited to the wedding?"

"No, they weren't. And since you know why, can you blame her?"

He nods, but doesn't say anything. I'm sure he has to maintain a level of professionalism.

After going over several more questions with me, he steps out of the room. Immediately, I stand, pacing again and it seems like forever before he steps back into the room.

"Hey Bennett, you're good to go. If you follow me, I'll take you out to the waiting area where your friends are."

I follow him down a few hallways to the waiting area where I find Phoenix, Axel, Cash, and Cole, along with their wives.

"Willow's not out yet?" I ask.

"No, and Jack is back there as well. I don't know if he's with her or if he's talking to someone else," Axel says.

Even though I try to sit down, I can't sit still, and begin pacing again. I need to know that she's okay, and to be there to offer her comfort. This can't be easy for her.

"This is a lot like what happened with me and Emelie," Axel says, trying to calm me.

"Only with us it was my ex-boyfriend, not a family member," Emelie says. "But the cops were great at handling it, so I'm sure they will do well with this too."

While I know that they're trying to offer comfort, it all means nothing. Until I have my wife back in my arms safe and sound, where I can protect her and make sure that she's taken care of, then I'll relax.

Chapter 21

Willow

I really don't want to be here in this room. All I can think about is Bennett. Where is he? Is he okay and what type of questions are they asking him? When the detective steps into the room, I feel like I'm going to be sick to my stomach.

"As you know, you're here because your uncle gave a statement that he believes you are being held against your will. This is to assess your safety and well-being. Everything you say in this room is between us and you are safe here."

Stopping myself from rolling my eyes, as I've not felt safe near cops for a while. Especially back home where my uncle could control them.

"How did you meet Bennett?" he starts off.

"I met my husband online," I answer, correcting him.

"And what made you decide to move out here with a man that you met online?"

"Well, after my uncle tried to rape me, the cops in Chicago refused to do anything, I no longer felt safe. I was going to leave regardless, but it seemed better to go somewhere where someone actually wanted me." I can't stop the bite in my tone.

"Were there police reports filed and if so, where?"

"Yes, I tried multiple times, but when your uncle is a big politician and has the cops in his pockets, they get swept under the rug." As he takes down notes, I give him the information that I remember about who I talked to and when and where.

"And when you got here, you married Bennett right away for protection?"

I stop and just stare at him because nothing I have said so far has come anything close to that.

"You're putting words into my mouth. I did not marry Bennett for protection. I married him because I love him. Before I came here, we talked for quite a while. Then once I arrived, we dated. We went to the rodeo, had dinner with his friends, we were each other's dates to Cash and Hope's wedding, all before we got married ourselves."

"So why would your uncle think you're being held against your will?"

"He doesn't really think that. What he's doing is manipulating the truth to get me away from my husband so he can force me to stop telling what he did to me. Not only did he break into our cabin, but he's been making threats left and right. Nor did I give him a forwarding address or any information. Yet he still found me. How?"

He scribbles down notes and asks me a few questions about different ways that I might have slipped up and my uncle might have found me. All in all, I feel like the questions are ridiculous at this point. The more questions he asks, the more irritated I get.

Finally, he steps out, and it's just me alone in the room again. All I can think about is my husband and how he is doing and if he's okay. It seems like I sit in that room forever before the detective is back.

"All right, I have a few more questions that I need to ask given the nature of the complaint," he says, actually looking sorry.

"By all means continue to put words in my mouth." I roll my eyes because at this point I'm just done.

He looks at me almost apologetically.

"Sorry, I guess I'm more stressed than I realized." I mutter before he continues.

"Has Bennett in any way put his hands on you in anger or any way that you were not comfortable with?"

"He is not that kind of man. Of course he didn't."

"Has Bennett ever forced himself on you?"

"No, it was my uncle that tried to force himself on me."

"Were you coerced into marrying Bennett for any reason?"

"No."

He nods, and again looks apologetic before stepping out of the room once more. But this time he's only gone for a minute or two before coming back in.

"All right, you are free to go. If you will follow me, I'll take you to the waiting room where your friends are."

"Where's Bennett?" I ask not moving from the room.

"Your husband is already waiting for you," he says.

I swear I've never moved so fast in my life. The moment I see my husband in the waiting room full on relief hits me. It's followed by a wall of pure exhaustion.

I can tell the moment he sees me because he quits pacing and his body relaxes. Without stopping, I walk right into his arms and only then do I finally and truly calm down. I feel safe again and I realize that he's okay, too.

"Are you all right, sweetheart?"

I nod, because he's here now, and that makes everything perfect.

When I sway a little, he wastes no time picking me up and carrying me out to the truck. All of our friends follow, but I don't hear anything they say. Instead, I snuggle into his chest and let him take control because I think he needs it as much as I need to let him.

Placing me gently in the truck, he puts the seat buckle on me and gets in. Then we make our way home. I don't remember the drive or even falling asleep, but the next thing I know, he's opening the truck door and carrying me inside.

Once in the house, he heads straight for our bedroom and lays me down on the bed. A moment later, he's crawling into bed with me and pulling me against his chest, holding me tight.

Neither of us moves as we lie there soaking each other in and enjoying the comfort that we're both all right. Whatever tomorrow might bring, we're both ready because we have each other.

· · · · • · • · · ·

Bennett

It's been a few days since we were at the police station and thankfully or unfortunately, things have been quiet depending on how you want to look at it. I'm still completely on edge waiting for whatever her uncle decides to try next. I won't be happy until he's either six feet under or locked away for life.

The guys have been great with any help we need. We all agree that we don't want Willow living in fear. Whether I decide to take matters into my own hands or not, I know they would be there to help me.

The problem is I'm not quite sure what to do. While I won't leave her side or leave her vulnerable, I do need to figure out a game plan.

Detective Greer said that her uncle can get in trouble for filing a false police report, but the problem is the police on his end can make that go away fairly easily. If he is charged with filing a false police report, it's at most a year in jail back in Chicago, but if he's caught here, it's only six months. What I want is for him to go to jail, and not have a chance to get out.

Most of all, I want him to go to jail here in Montana because the men here won't put up with a man who tried to rape a woman, especially his own niece. It'll satisfy me knowing justice will be served behind prison bars above and beyond his sentence.

This morning I'm out back chopping wood. The nights are starting to get cooler, so we've been lighting a fire at night. If I didn't have

Willow living here, I wouldn't have started using fire wood so early, and would have more than enough stocked up. But she likes to curl up and snuggle by the fire, and I sure as hell am not saying no to that. So I figured I'd spend the morning chopping some more firewood to make sure that we have plenty.

Also, I can get some great thinking done with all the manual labor and I'm hoping maybe an idea or even the spark of one will come to me.

Cole is meeting with a buddy he served with who just moved to the mountain after finishing his last deployment. He said he'd fill him in on what is going on with Willow and her uncle. I figure it can't hurt to have another helping hand. Cole says his buddy is an excellent tracker, just like he is and he has some good military connections, so I guess I'm hoping for a miracle.

The longer I go without an idea, the more frustrated I get and the more I take it out on the wood. Before long, I'm lost in my own thoughts and have a powerful rhythm going. Then all of a sudden, a blood-curdling scream fills the air.

Chapter 22

Willow

Bennett's outside chopping wood, and I know he's frustrated with everything going on with my uncle. Apparently, he's getting those frustrations out by chopping wood. I'm spying on him, hoping he won't catch me because I'm enjoying the view. Holy hell, watching those muscles ripple while he's shirtless and cutting wood, it's not only breathtaking but a damn turn on.

The sweat on his body and the way he swings that ax make the tattoos on his arms move and flex and is sexy as hell. The fact that this man is all mine, just adds to his hotness factor.

I'm on my second cup of coffee when there's a knock at the door. I assume it's Emelie because she said she was going to come over today for us to do some quilting together while our husbands chat.

Not even thinking twice, I open the door. Only it's not Emelie and Axel on the other side. It's my aunt.

"How did you find..." I start and don't get to finish.

"No, you listen here you ungrateful brat. You need to stop telling lies about your uncle. Right this minute, you need to go back to the police station and tell them you made it all up," she seethes.

Is this woman serious?

"I didn't make any of it up."

"This has gotten out of hand. You're responsible for him losing his job, for the cops turning on him, and for the rumors that are now flying back home. Apparently, because your story got out, other girls think they can take advantage of him too," my aunt snarls.

Other girls have come out of the woodwork? Well, that means that I wasn't the only one he tried to pull this bullshit on. Now that I have that information, it's enough for me to never back down, no matter what the cost. A man like him can't be allowed to continue doing this to innocent women.

"So, you're perfectly fine being married to a pedophile and a rapist just so long as no one knows about it," I sass back.

That's the moment I see my uncle step around the corner of the house. Was he purposely hiding out of eyesight?

"I'm going to teach you what happens to girls like you. Just remember I gave you the chance to change your story, and now there will be no more chances." He lunges for me, and I let out a scream at the top of my lungs praying my husband will hear.

I watch as his hands sail towards my face, connecting with my cheek. The pain is delayed for a second and then the side of my face feels like it's on fire.

While he's trying to pull me towards his car, I'm gripping on to the doorway as hard as possible. Thinking to myself there has to be something that I can get to within reach. Unfortunately, the shotgun is too far from the door and if I let go, he'll easily overpower me.

Hoping to connect with one of them and get them enough off balance to give me a few seconds advantage, I kick my feet.

"Leave me alone!" I scream at the top of my lungs.

One minute I'm struggling and fighting both of them off, and then the next there's a loud growl. When an axe goes flying in the air and pierces the driver-side door of their car, it causes them both to freeze and start yelling.

"What the fuck was that?" my uncle yells.

That's the moment Bennett rounds the corner at a full on run and tackles my uncle to the ground. Using the distraction, I lunge and grab the shotgun, but I can't get a clear shot without the possibility of hurting Bennett.

I'm so focused on the fight in front of me between my uncle and Bennett that I don't notice my aunt coming at me until she tries to take the shotgun.

Now she's got a grip on it, and I fight her for it. When she pushes the barrel up into the air, I'm hoping to pull it down and fire a shot at her. Hopefully, that should distract my uncle enough to give Bennett the advantage.

But my aunt is stronger than someone her size should be. Or maybe we're just running on adrenaline. With all my might, I try pushing her back, getting her off balance and making her stumble off the porch, but I'm not able to move her. While I desperately want to look over at Bennett and make sure he's okay, I don't dare take my eyes off of my own fight.

"Just give up, little girl," my aunt growls.

For some odd reason, her words trigger me to start laughing, which catches her off guard. It's enough for me to push her back a few inches.

"I will never stop talking and telling my story. Now that it's out and public, if I go missing that will make you look guilty. Who do you think will be the first suspects? And if you think my husband or my friends will allow it, you need to think again. You're not getting out of this, and the fact that you support your husband after all he's done, well, you're just as guilty as he is." I laugh again, mostly because I love how irritated she gets when I do. Hell, maybe it's not the right thing to do, but I'm out of options at the moment.

I guess my laughter enrages her because she builds up enough steam to slam me back against the wall of the house. The logs hit me at an odd angle and a piercing pain shoots down my back. I'm definitely going to have a bruise there tomorrow.

She uses that moment to get an advantage. Remembering something my dad always said about using momentum against someone, I'm able to flip her to the side and get my back from against the wall.

Everything seems to be happening in slow motion, but at the same time my brain is not registering every movement. Suddenly, she's twisting and turning the gun, causing me to lose my grip. Once again, I try to use some of that momentum to get her off balance.

When she slams me back against the porch railing, I'm able to put her off before she smashes me back again. Only this time, I lose my balance. No matter how hard I try to grip the railing or anything around me, it's as if it all vanishes into thin air as I fall backward, my feet go over my head and I hit the ground.

The air is knocked out of me, and for a moment I feel weightless before the world around me turns blurry and then goes black.

Chapter 23

Bennett

I hate hospitals. I hate doctors. I hate the smell of whatever they use to clean this place. I hate the nurses who keep looking at me like I'm going to attack them.

Actually, the last one might happen as I'm up and pacing in the waiting room. After Willow fell, her aunt and uncle got a little too cocky. I was able to knock her uncle out and get the shotgun away from her aunt and restrain her.

When Willow wouldn't wake up, I knew I had to get her to a doctor. My first call was to the guys, and then Detective Greer. Axel and Emelie stayed with the aunt and uncle while I brought her to the hospital. All our friends met me here, along with Greer, who is now questioning me about what happened.

"Bennett, I know there's a lot going on, but I need you to start from the beginning and tell me exactly what transpired," he says.

Then Greer and the guy standing next to him get their pen and paper out to take notes.

I look over at Jack, who Phoenix thankfully thought to call. Apparently, he beat the police here to the hospital.

"Just tell them the truth," Jack says.

Nodding, I begin. "I was out back chopping wood, so I didn't hear or see anyone pull up the driveway. When I heard Willow scream, I came running, and that's when I saw her uncle had his hands on her. She was gripping the doorway, presumably trying to prevent him from dragging her off to his car.

After I yelled to get their attention, I threw my axe at his driver's side door. The distraction gave Willow enough time to grab the shotgun while I got her uncle away from her.

Then her aunt began struggling for the shotgun. Though I'm not a hundred percent sure how that happened because her uncle started fighting me. When her aunt pushed her back against the porch rail, Willow lost her balance and fell backward and landed on the ground.

That was enough of a distraction that I was able to knock the uncle out, detain the aunt, and get the gun away from her."

Finishing up, I tell them what the uncle was saying about her needing to shut up about the lies, how Willow had told them that she wasn't going to stop telling the truth, and how her uncle had told me that he had planned to kill us both.

Detective Greer asks more questions and every so often his partner asks me to repeat some things. This irritates me because all I want to do is see my wife. She's back behind the emergency room doors and I have no idea if she's okay, if she's awake, or if she's scared. It's killing me.

By the time we got to the hospital, she was just starting to wake up and then she passed out again. They rushed her back through the emergency room doors and that was the last I saw of her, and I haven't heard anything either. All the guys and their wives are here in the emergency room with me when a man I've never seen before walks in with several bags of food.

When Cole jumps up and greets him, the man hesitantly walks over to our group, his eyes constantly scanning the room. He's tall and buff, and his arms are covered in scars.

"Guys, this is my buddy, Storm. We served together, and he just moved to the mountain on the other side of me," Cole says.

Storm just nods at the introduction. Though if Cole served with him during his third time and trusts him, then the rest of us do well as well. Up on the mountain, we band together and have our own little community. He has his own reasons for coming out here, as we all do, but that doesn't mean that he has to do it alone.

Cole introduces Storm to everybody, but he doesn't speak until he gets to me.

"Sorry about your girl. Any updates?" he asks.

"Not yet," I tell him, and he nods and grabs a chair next to Cole and his wife, Jana.

Not bothering to try to sit down, I continue pacing the waiting room. When one of the nurses makes eye contact with me, I finally snap.

"You're seriously going to look at me and tell me there are no updates on my wife?" I ask her, making her eyes go wide.

Instantly, Phoenix's wife Jenna is at my side.

"May I?" she asks, and I nod.

Jenna goes up to the nurse and they whisper so that I don't hear what is being said. With the way they are nodding their heads, I'm praying that means good news.

"Thank you," Jenna finally says.

The nurse looks over her shoulder and gives me an apologetic smile.

"So, she is awake and asking for you, but they had to take her back for a CT scan on her head.

In just a few minutes, she'll be going back to her room, and a nurse will come and take you to her. For now, that's all the nurse knows," Jenna says.

It has to be a good sign that Willow's awake and asking for me. Anything else that shows up on the test we can deal with later. If I'm at her side holding her hand, I know that I can handle this so much better.

What seems like forever, but in reality, was probably only a few minutes, finally a nurse leads me back to Willow. I have every intention of rushing to her, picking her up into my arms and holding her. Yet when I step through the door and see all the wires attached to her, I stopped short.

Seeing me, she gives me one of her breathtaking smiles.

"Bennett." She sighs and holds her hand up for me.

Like it's a magnet, and I can't say no, I'm drawn to her. Taking her hand in mine, I'm comforted because that contact alone is reassuring and calming.

"Why so many wires?" I ask staring, trying to figure out what they all are.

"They're just a lot of monitors, but I do have something to tell you. Why don't you sit down?" Willow says.

Even though there's a smile on her face, I'm instantly nervous.

Grabbing the chair nearest to her bed, I pull it up as close as I can. Then I sit, taking her hand in mine. More than ever, I need the skin to skin contact with her.

"When I got here, the doctors ran all sorts of tests and I'm not sure what all came back, but they did tell me one thing. Something good to hopefully come out of all this. I'm pregnant." She bites her bottom lip and looks nervous, as if this isn't the most amazing news that I've heard in my whole life.

My wife is pregnant and giving me a child! Yeah, that's great news, life-changing. We're going to build our own family up on the mountain and our child will grow up with our friends' kids. As my whole life flashes before my eyes, I lean in and place a soft kiss on her cheek. Then gently place my hand over her lower stomach, right where our little peanut is growing.

There are so many things that I want to say, but only one word seems to come out of my mouth: "*pregnant.*"

I'm still in complete disbelief, not to mention speechless, but she smiles and nods. Bringing our joined hands up, I kiss them gently. I had absolutely no idea that she was pregnant. Though looking back, little things that I wrote off as stress could have been a sign, and I vow to pay more and better attention to her.

Slowly, each of the other couples comes to visit.

"Only two visitors are allowed in a room at a time." The nurse who looks fresh out of nursing school pokes her head in and tells us.

"Well, I guess it's a good thing there are only two visitors. Since I'm her husband and I'm not leaving her side, then these two are visiting her," I say, referring to Cash and Hope.

The nurse opens her mouth to say something else, but then thinks better of it and moves on.

They keep Willow in the hospital overnight, and the next morning Axel and Emelie are there with food.

"We figured you weren't leaving until she did, and hospital breakfasts are horrible, so we brought some food for both of you," Emelie says, handing over the bag.

It's great to have friends that know you sometimes better than you know yourself.

· · • • • • • • · ·

Willow

I'm finally being released from the hospital, and I couldn't be more thrilled. Honestly, I'm looking forward to a solid night of sleep without being constantly woken up by a noise in the hallway or someone coming in to check on me.

Of course, Bennett has been super careful with me. He insists on taking me out in a wheelchair to the front door where he has his truck waiting. Then he won't even let my feet touch the ground, lifting me from the wheelchair into the seat and buckling me up.

Even though I love that he's so caring and gentle, I hope he doesn't plan on being this way the entire pregnancy. Otherwise it's going to be an extremely long nine months.

All the way home, he holds my hand, never letting go. When we arrive, he tries to stop me from getting out of the truck. But that's when I have to finally put my foot down.

"I feel fine, and while I do, I would like to walk on my own two feet. Though I promise if I don't feel good, I'll let you carry me wherever your heart desires. But right now, I would like to walk, please." I say it gently as possible and I can see the conflict in his eyes before he finally nods.

Trying to offer him some comfort, I slip my arm through his so I can use it as support. Not that I need it, but I know it makes him feel better, so I do it. Once I'm safely on the couch with more blankets and pillows than I could ever want, he heads to the kitchen to make me lunch.

Returning, he says, "Here are the prenatal vitamins the doctor told you to take, but Emelie said they taste gross, so there's some juice to take with it. I've made your lunch with fruits and vegetables, everything that the doctor recommends that you need to eat." Then he sets a plate with an enormous amount of food down on the coffee table in front of me. There's more than I'm pretty sure even he could eat in one sitting.

"You're going to help me eat all this, right? Just because I'm eating for two, doesn't mean that I'm going to have anywhere near your appetite."

Sitting down next to me, he holds the plate for both of us to slowly eat our lunch. Though he only takes one bite for every two of mine, it's something. When we're finished eating, he cleans up the mess and sits next to me, resting his head in my lap. Then, turning to face my nonexistent baby bump, he places a kiss there.

"Now we should start thinking about baby names," he says, and I just laugh.

"We have no idea if it's a boy or a girl, and we just found out I'm pregnant. We've got time."

"I can't wait to decorate the baby's room." He smiles and takes my hand in his.

As we make plans, he slowly runs his thumb over my wedding ring. Bennett started doing that in the hospital and I don't think he realizes he does it, but it's a little thing that I love so much.

"Are you happy? Is this what you truly want now that your aunt and uncle are out of the way?" he asks.

I turn his head to make sure he's looking at me.

"This is absolutely what I want. Yes, I ran from them, but without realizing it, I was running toward you. I fell in love with you, and I'm not going anywhere unless you push me away."

"I'm not pushing you away. I plan to hold you as tight as you will let me."

"As tight as you want. I love you," I whisper.

"I love you too, sweetheart. Always."

Epilogue

Willow

Fuck, I'm sore, but in the best possible way. Having just given birth to our son a few hours ago, this is the first time that I've had a moment of rest. When I doze off for just a bit, I wake up to the most beautiful sight. Bennett is lying on the couch with our son on his chest fast asleep.

This big, burly, bearded, tattooed mountain man is snuggling with our tiny, innocent little baby, and it's just the sweetest sight I could ever imagine. Luckily, my cell phone is on the table beside my bed and I'm able to snap a few pictures before he looks over at me.

"We need to get several cameras to keep around the house because we're going to need them," I tell him.

After taking more than a few pictures, he has a big, goofy smile on his face.

"Anything you want, my wife," he says, turning to kiss the top of our son's head.

"You've got to stop doing that. I just gave birth to him, and you're already somehow turning me on."

The doctor said we couldn't have sex again for six to eight weeks depending on how I heal, so being turned on before I'm even released from the hospital is extremely inconvenient.

"Then you better stop looking at me like that. The doctor said I can't touch you and if it means putting your health at risk, then it's not worth it."

When it comes to my health, Bennett is extra vigilant. Whatever the doctor said while I was pregnant, he had enforced. There was a list of food I wasn't supposed to eat. Every time we saw the doctor, he made sure that I was allowed to be up and around.

Thankfully, my doctor just laughed it off. She thought it was great how protective and involved he was

"I'm simply looking at my husband snuggling my son. And just because you can't touch me, doesn't mean I can't touch you." I send him a flirty wink, and he groans.

"Baby, if you're not cumming for the next six to eight weeks, then neither am I."

"There's no need for you to suffer."

"Sweetheart, you just gave birth to our son. It's the most amazing gift you could have ever given me. So, it's absolutely nothing for me to wait with you." The sincerity in his voice puts a stop to any fight I had left in me.

"Now get some sleep. Soon our friends will want to visit and meet our son."

It wasn't our plan to give birth in the hospital, but Bennett wanted to take me away for one last weekend before the baby got here, but the baby had other ideas and decided to make a slightly early appearance. After Bennett told Phoenix, he spread the word, and they all decided they couldn't wait and were going to come and visit. I'll be in the hospital for the next few days, so it will be nice to see them.

The weekend away was a celebration that we were free. My aunt and uncle won't be getting out of jail anytime soon. They were charged with attempted kidnapping, multiple assault charges, filing a false police report, and a few other charges in regard to myself and Bennett. Now they are being sent back to Chicago to face trial for multiple rape charges and other crimes that have come to light.

Needless to say, they will be sentenced to many lifetimes in jail and it's such a relief.

I manage to get a cat nap in before there is a knock on my door.

"Oh, we didn't mean to wake you," Jana says and she, her husband Cole, and their friend, Storm come in.

Over the last several months, we've all gotten to know Storm pretty well. He's easily fit in as one of the group, not that Cole has given him much of a choice. But he has come out of his shell for us.

Slowly, the rest of the guys and their families pile in to meet the newest addition to the clan.

"Now that we are all here, what is this little guy's name?" Hope asks, holding him and looking at him with love in her eyes.

"We named him William, after Willow's dad," Bennett says, as tears fill my eyes.

Without me even asking him, Bennett told me his name. It felt right and couldn't be a more perfect fit.

"Well, since everyone is here, I have something to tell you all, too." Storm says, catching all our attention.

Jana gives him a look and rubs his arm. I get the feeling this isn't super happy news.

"Everything okay?" Emelie asks because she apparently got the same feeling.

"I was just notified that one of the guys that I served with was killed in action. He's a really good friend of mine and I had made him a promise that if anything were to happen to him, I would take care of his wife. Before he left for deployment, they found out she was pregnant.

Neither of them have any family. So, after talking with her, we decided that she's going to join me here on the mountain, at least until after the baby's born and she gets on her feet. Tomorrow I'll leave to go to the funeral and help her pack and take care of everything."

Something in my gut says that our family is about to grow by two more. I know he says it is temporary, but I don't think it is.

Whatever happens, I know we will welcome her with open arms.

· · · · ● · ● · · ·

Want a Bonus Epilogue of Bennett and Willow. **Sign up for my Newsletter to get it!**

Want Storm's story? Get it in **Take Me To The Edge**

Other Books by Kaci Rose

See all of Kaci Rose's Books

Oakside Military Heroes Series

Saving Noah – Lexi and Noah

Saving Easton – Easton and Paisley

Saving Teddy – Teddy and Mia

Saving Levi – Levi and Mandy

Saving Gavin – Gavin and Lauren

Saving Logan – Logan and Faith

Oakside Shorts

Saving Mason - Mason and Paige

Saving Ethan – Bri and Ethan

Mountain Men of Whiskey River

Take Me To The River – Axel and Emelie

Take Me To The Cabin – Pheonix and Jenna

Take Me To The Lake – Cash and Hope

Taken by The Mountain Man - Cole and Jana

Take Me To The Mountain – Bennett and Willow

Take Me To The Edge – Storm

Mountain Men of Mustang Mountain

(Series Written with Dylann Crush and Eve London)

February is for Ford – Ford and Luna

Club Red – Short Stories

Daddy's Dare – Knox and Summer

Sold to my Ex's Dad - Evan and Jana

Jingling His Bells – Zion and Emma

Club Red: Chicago

Elusive Dom

Chasing the Sun Duet

Sunrise – Kade and Lin

Sunset – Jasper and Brynn

Rock Stars of Nashville

She's Still The One – Dallas and Austin

Standalone Books

Texting Titan - Denver and Avery

Accidental Sugar Daddy – Owen and Ellie

Stay With Me Now – David and Ivy

Midnight Rose - Ruby and Orlando

Committed Cowboy – Whiskey Run Cowboys

Stalking His Obsession - Dakota and Grant

Falling in Love on Route 66 - Weston and Rory

Billionaire's Marigold - Mari and Dalton

Connect with Kaci Rose

Website

Facebook

Kaci Rose Reader's Facebook Group

TikTok

Instagram

Twitter

Goodreads

Book Bub

Join Kaci Rose's VIP List (Newsletter)

Please Leave a Review!

I love to hear from my readers! Please **head over to your favorite store and leave a review** of what you thought of this book!

About Kaci Rose

Kaci Rose writes steamy contemporary romance mostly set in small towns. She grew up in Florida but longs for the mountains over the beach.

She is a mom to 5 kids and a dog who is scared of his own shadow.

She also writes steamy cowboy romance as Kaci M. Rose.

Printed in Poland
by Amazon Fulfillment
Poland Sp. z o.o., Wrocław